Cute for a Black Girl

By Amy Watkins

To all the girls who have yet to realize how beautiful they truly are.
Know that you are God's masterpiece.

"I praise you, for I am fearfully and wonderfully made. Wonderful are your works; my soul knows it very well."
Psalm 139:14 ESV

Prologue

I was so excited. It had been almost a year since I was on a date. I blamed it mainly on the COVID crisis, although some of my reclusiveness was my fault too. I met Taylor online. She hearted and commented a very controversial post I tweeted about God and homosexuality. When I posted it, I didn't expect to get many likes, but her comment really caught my eye, "How can I judge a gay man when I sin too?" I looked at her profile as a result. Her picture was beautiful. She was a long-haired brunette with green eyes and freckles. Physical fitness was obviously important to her like me. And from the look of her profile, we had a lot in common. Our mom's both died when we were young, our fathers were both bigots, we were raised in small towns, and as soon as we turned eighteen, we both migrated to the big city in search of a more adventurous life.

I took a deep breath and sent her a message and to my utter surprise, she responded that day. We tweeted, texted, and talked over the next few months and when the social isolation restrictions were lifted, we made plans to meet at a park not too far from my apartment.

I brushed my hair and put on my most flattering outfit.

"Ohhh weee!" my roommate and best friend complimented me. I gazed in the mirror making sure no strand of hair was out of place. "That girl better watch out. She might fall in love as soon as she sees you."

I laughed. The comment helped to ease my nerves.

"I hope this date goes well considering my last disastrous relationship," I responded rolling my eyes.

"Yeah, but that's old news. I mean we were in high school. We both did a bunch of dumb stuff in high school. It made us stronger though."

"Yeah," I agreed.

"It's about time you move on and get back out in that dating field. Just have fun. Don't worry about finding your soulmate. Just enjoy getting to know someone."

"Yeah, you're right!" I nodded.

My roommate wished me good luck and gave me a hug as we parted ways. I jumped in my car and started on the five-mile journey that may very well have been the beginning of the rest of my life. I loved the rev of my sports car's engine, especially as I shifted gears. I only had my car for three years, but I had driven her hard during that time. Lots of long road trips with my friends, lots of street racing, a few accidents, and not to mention the full out assault that my ex-girlfriend executed shortly after our breakup. Nevertheless, the car still purred like a kitten. Her ride was still smooth and solid.

I stopped at the grocery store and purchased a single rose and then walked across the street to the park where I was scheduled to meet my potential next girlfriend. I was early so I sat on a bench and waited as I watched couples walking hand-in-hand and mothers jogging while pushing baby carriages. Then I saw her. She wore tight white jeans and a loose turquoise shirt that really complimented her eyes.

"Taylor?" I asked.

"Hi!" She looked as nervous as I felt, but her meekness was a turn-on for me.

"You look even more beautiful in person."

"So, do you," Taylor responded.

I handed her the rose and we talked, laughed, and joked for hours. The day was easily turning into the best date I had ever been on.

"So, what is your biggest regret?" Taylor asked.

"Oh goodness," I responded as I brushed my hand down my face, "You sure you ready to hear all that?"

"Yeah, I mean I want us to be open and honest with each other. I want to know all your secrets. And I want you to know mine."

"Okay, well…You know my best friend is female right?"

"Right?"

"Well, one day I made a move on her. I tried to kiss her; but she wasn't feeling me in that way. Oh, it was so embarrassing. And it scared me half to death. I thought I had lost her as a friend. We are cool now; but boy-o-boy did I regret that one."

Taylor laughed. It wasn't a mean laugh. It was more of an "oh your innocence is so cute" laugh.

"So…wait, are you still crushing on your bestie?"

"Oh no. I mean, don't get me wrong. My best friend is pretty. But I prefer girls with green eyes," I said as I winked. Taylor blushed. "Okay so your turn. What is your biggest regret?"

"Well," she said as she snuggled close to me and told her story in almost a whisper, "When I was younger, I wasn't sure what I liked. I dated all kinds of people. Black, White, Hispanic, whoever. I was about seventeen and I was sleeping around with this Black guy I went to school with. I'd usually sneak him into my house and we'd...you know. Well one day my dad caught us, and you know how my dad is. He has a horrible temper. I feared him so...I said it was rape."

"What?!" I was horrified, but Taylor was still smiling.

"Yeah, it was stupid. I regret it with all my heart. But I can't keep living in the past. I had to forgive myself and forget about the whole incident. You know what really sucks? I still have trouble confronting my dad. I'm twenty-one years old now, and I still can't tell him I like what I like."

"Well did you tell him you lied about the rape?"

"No! He'd kill me if he ever found out I was willingly sleeping with a Black guy."

"So, what happened to the guy?"

"He ended up in jail. I haven't heard from him since."

"What?! Is he still in jail?"

"Last I heard he was. He was sentenced to life in prison."

"And you didn't think to tell the truth? You didn't think to go to the courthouse, the police, or the judge and tell them he was innocent?"

"I was seventeen. I was scared..."

"And what do you think he was? He was seventeen too."

Taylor looked puzzled as if she never considered this young Black boy's feelings. As if she never realized that she ruined an innocent man's life.

"I can't...I can't..." I mentioned as I shook my head and walked away.

"Wait, where are you going? Things were really going well before I told you that story. Can't we just forget about it and pick up where we left off?"

"You just don't get it do you? My best friend is Black. I love her like I love myself. Her brother is my brother. If anything like that happened to her or her brother, I'd...I'd...die! I can't be with anyone who caused an innocent person pain like that. Sorry, But I can't deal with you anymore."

Chapter 1 – William's Frost in 2018

I was swamped with paperwork. My desk was covered with the tales of many people's grievances and indiscretions. I was expecting a call from my seventeen-year-old daughter, Chloe. Every night at eight she was obligated to check in and assure me of her safety. It was 7:45 P.M and I wasn't even halfway done with my documents. Who knew that taking this job as a judge in this small Virginia town would be so overwhelming?

"Ring ring ring," my phone blared.

Good she's early, I thought as I picked up my phone only to see an unknown number.

I didn't have time for telemarketers, so I ignored the call and proceeded with my work.

Ten minutes later, "ring ring ring," form the same number as before. If it was a telemarketer, I planned to cuss them out.

"Hello!" I answered.

"Yes, may I speak to a Mr. William Wilcox?" a polite sounding woman responded.

"I'm not interested," I claimed then I pulled the phone away from my ear in attempt to hang up.

"No! No! Wait, Mr. Wilcox!" she stopped me.

I would have hung up, but I heard the urgency in her voice. Maybe it was important.

"Mr. Wilcox, this is RN Hamilton from Spotsy Regional Hospital. We have your daughter here."

"Chloe? Is she okay?"

"Ummm, sir, she's in critical condition. You may want to hurry and get down here as soon as possible. They are working on her now."

"What? What's wrong with her? What happened?"

"I don't have any further information at this time. Just try to get here, quickly," she said as she got off the phone.

My heart dropped. My only daughter was in the hospital in critical condition while I was sitting at work ignoring calls. I rose, grabbed my keys, my coat, and ran out the door. I hopped into my Mercedes and high tailed it down the long stretch of country road. I prayed the whole way, "Lord, I know I haven't been to church in a while, but please don't take my baby girl. I have lost so much. Please don't take her away too. If you save my baby, I promise I will return to church. I will return to you. Just please don't take my baby."

I pulled into Spotsy ER, parked the car illegally near the ambulance bay, and ran inside.

"May I help you?" said a young lady that stood behind the check in desk.

"Yes…my daughter…I got a call that she was here," I could barely breathe as I talked.

"Name?"

"Chloe Wilcox."

"Only family are allowed to see her at this time," the lady responded.

"Yes, I'm her dad."

She looked at me sideways and squinted. It was a look I had grown accustomed to when people saw Chloe and I together.

"But she's Black," the lady stated.

"Yes, and I'm White. But she's mine. Do you need to see the certificate, or can I go see my baby now?"

"Sir, I apologize. Please come follow me. I'll take you right to her."

She led me down a long hallway that bypassed the ER.

"Ma'am, I was told she's in the ER," I stated when the nurse walked past those double doors.

"She was in the ER. She's been moved to the ICU."

"The ICU?" Panic filled my heart. *Why was Chloe in the ICU? What happened? Was she okay?* A million thoughts ran through my head as I followed that lady down the hall, up the elevator and to a department marked in big black letters, "Intensive Care Unit."

The lady pressed an intercom located next to the doors of the unit.

"Yes," another lady answered from the intercom box.

"I have the father of Chloe Wilcox here to see her."

"Buzzzzz" the door sounded, and I walked through the doors where I was met by another nurse.

"Mr. Wilcox," she spoke.

"Yes."

"I'm Nurse Hamilton. We spoke over the phone."

"Yes."

"Right this way sir. Chloe is in room 3."

My knees were weak. I don't know how I managed the strength to put one foot in front of the other as I made my way behind Nurse Hamilton and to room three. I looked through the glass doors where my baby laid, and I paused in my tracks. There were all kinds of machines around her beeping, dripping, and blowing. Chloe laid there still and unresponsive.

"Come in," Nurse Hamilton said. "Don't be scared. Chloe needs you."

I stepped through the glass door and watched as a tube blew air into her mouth made her chest move up and down. Another tube ran from her nose draining black liquid. Her beautiful chocolate skin was an ashen gray.

"What happened?"

"The doctors think it was an overdose."

Tears started to run down my face as the nurse spoke.

"Her heart stopped. They did CPR on her for ten minutes before they could get her heart to start beating on its own again. They gave her a medication called Narcan. It helps people who have had drug overdoses. It worked. But they are still running labs to determine the cause of her cardiac arrest."

I walked over to Chloe, grabbed her hand, and stroked it. It was warm but limp.

"Here's a chair. You can sit with her if you like," The nurse pulled a chair next to Chloe's bed, and I sat without letting go of Chloe's hand. The nurse left, and the tears continued to flow. I looked at my beautiful girl. Her hair was a wild mane of tight curls just like it was on the day I met her eleven years ago. Then, I was a thirty-seven-year-old successful lawyer in Washington, DC. I worked for one of the most prestigious divorce law firms in the city. I had money, a house, a nice car, and respect. I had it made. But my heart was empty.

I had a strong desire to start my own family. The home I came from was broken. My dad left when I was two leaving my mother to struggle raising five children on a teacher's salary. It was hard, but my mother, being half Bengali and half Caucasian, was a strong woman who instilled great values in me and my siblings. She taught us hard work and discipline. We were all successful in our careers, but, not so much in our personal lives. You couldn't tell by looking at me that I was one fourth Indian because I favored my dad so much. You'd think my mom would have resentment towards me, but her heart was kind, and my looks didn't faze her.

In all my years of dating various women from various backgrounds, I hadn't found anyone that I wanted to spend the rest of my life with. They were either too pushy, too unmotivated, too loud, too quiet, too wild, too boring, or just not interested in me. At thirty-seven, I had damn near given up on my dreams of starting a family. But on Easter Sunday, my pastor inspired me.

"Religion that is pure and undefiled before God the Father is this: to visit orphans and widows in their affliction, and to keep oneself unstained from the world. James 1:27 ESV."

Orphans. It hit me like a ton of bricks. There were so many children without parents in America. They needed me, and I needed them. I went on an adoption website the next day and filled out an application. I was called by a case manager the day after and she walked me through the steps of becoming a parent.

After four months of parenting classes, home visits, and preparation, I became a licensed foster parent and was ready to open up my home to a future son or daughter. I walked around my first child matching event not expecting much. I figured it would take two or three events to find the right kid for me. There were hopeful children and potential parents running around everywhere. It was loud and overwhelming. I didn't engage with anyone initially. I just strolled through the chaos and observed.

In the midst, I noticed a presence following me. I stopped and turned my head to see my pursuer. She was a beautiful young round-faced girl. She had smooth chocolate skin and wild curly hair. Her light brown eyes were bright and engaging. She stopped when I stopped and smiled when I looked at her. Her smile revealed deep dimples in each cheek.

I took a few more steps forward and she followed. I turned again and she stopped and smiled again. I took quicker steps and she followed at the same pace. I stopped and turned around.

"Hi!" I enthusiastically spoke.

She didn't say anything. She just smiled.

I went over to her and got down on one knee extending my hand, "Hi, I'm William. What's your name?"

She didn't say anything nor did she grabbed my hand. She just smiled then skipped away taking my heart right away with her.

I continued to stroll around often feeling the presence of a gazing brown eyed, wild haired girl nearby. I'd see her face poking out behind a column or from the other side of the table. Whenever, I'd turn to look at her, she'd silently smile.

"Who's that girl?" I asked one of the case workers.

"Oh, that's Chloe. She's a sweet girl, but she's a handful. She doesn't talk."

"Is there something wrong with her? I mean is there a reason she can't talk? Like a disability or something?"

"Does it matter?" she asked in a judgy way.

"No, I was just curious."

It didn't matter to me one way or the other. I knew that a lot of children in foster care had disabilities or traumatic pasts. But they were all children of God and in need of love and support. I was ready to take on the challenge of adopting a child and all of the baggage that I'd expected would come with them.

"Selective mutism."

"Selective what?" I asked. I had never heard of the condition before.

"Selective mutism. There's nothing wrong with her voice or her hearing. She just chooses not to talk. She's been here for one year and hasn't said a word."

"Hmmm, I wonder why not?"

"Chloe is young, but she has a very traumatic past. Her mom's a drug addict. Chloe was born addicted to cocaine and heroin. And her dad abused her. He physically and sexually abused Chloe until her rescue by child services last year."

"Sexual abuse! But she's only, what like four or five years old?"

"Chloe is six and yes, sexual abuse. I know it's shocking. We think he started abusing her at age three but we're not sure. A neighbor called child protective services one night after hearing screams from Chloe's room. CPS found Chloe battered and broken. She was taken to the hospital where it was determined that there was sexual and physical trauma. Both parents were arrested and remain in jail currently."

I was appalled that so much could happen to someone so young. I was impressed at Chloe's resilience. She wasn't broken, she was smiling and pursuing. I wanted to be Chloe's hero. I wanted to show her that this world was not all bad. I wanted to show her the love and support that my mother had blessed me with.

"I want her," I said to the case manager.

She smiled at me and went into an office to start the paperwork.

It was a Saturday the first day Chloe stepped foot in my house. I could tell she was nervous. She clung onto the case workers leg like it was the only rooted tree during a tsunami. Chloe wasn't smiling, and the only part of her I could see peeking out from behind the social worker's leg was that curly hair and one brown eye.

All I could think was, *what did I get myself into?*

The caseworker must have sensed my reserve, "It'll take some getting used to, but I know this is going to work out just fine."

I nodded my head in agreement though I wasn't too sure. I extended my hand out to Chloe, and she gripped the social workers leg tighter.

"It's okay Chloe. He's not going to bite," she mentioned while attempting to escape from Chloe's death grip on her leg.

Chloe reluctantly loosened her hold and walked over to a corner in my living room. The social worker left, and it was just me and Chloe standing in silence staring awkwardly at each other. Both scared shitless.

I can do this.

"So, I heard your favorite food is pizza. I have some cooking in the oven if you're hungry."

Chloe just started crying. I didn't know what to do. I worried that if I touched her, she'd scream bloody murder thinking I was trying to hurt her. If I ignored her, would that be neglect?

"Chloe, please don't cry. Pizza is yummy." I tried to comfort her, but she just screamed louder.

I called the social worker. "Ummm somethings wrong. She's crying."

The social worker laughed, "Welcome to fatherhood. Congratulations."

"But what do I do?"

"Patience. Chloe has been through a lot. But just be kind and patient. She will come around soon."

Okay. Patience. Understanding. Kindness. I can do this.

I grabbed the pizza from the oven and sliced it. I put one on the plate for me and another for Chloe. I sat both plates on the table. I sat and took a bite of my own.

"Mmmm this pizza sure is yummy. I love pizza too you know."

Chloe cried louder.

"You sure you don't want to try it. It may make you feel better."

Chloe stopped crying and looked at me sideways. She huffed a little and wiped her tears away. She slowly made her way over to the table. She grabbed her plate and went back over to her corner of the room. Then she sat on the floor and took a bite.

I heard her breath out a sigh of relief, then she destroyed the rest of the pizza like a hungry lion cub feasting on a carcass. When she was done, she looked up at me, tomato sauce all over her face and smiled. She held up her plate.

"You want some more? You're a hungry little thing, aren't you?"

She didn't say a word and just held up her plate.

"Okay, you can have some more. But this time, you have to eat it at the table," I said reflecting on the foster parent classes I had taken and there emphasis on boundaries and discipline.

Chloe looked at me sideways again. I could tell she was pondering my offer.

She got up, sat at the table, and smiled.

I put another slice of pizza on her plate and we ate together, our first night as a family.

Chapter 2 – Chloe's Autumn in 2007

I didn't remember much about my life prior to meeting William. Every once in a while, I'd get flash backs from my past, men coming in and out of our house, a fly tickling my nose on a hot summer's day as I laid on the couch in our apartment which had no air conditioning, chomping down on Frostee Os as I watched cartoons on an old TV. Just bits and pieces of memories would occasionally invade my thoughts.

I remembered my mother vaguely. She slept a lot during the day; but she was nice to me. She'd let me watch cartoons all day while she slept. She had a lot of male friends. They'd give her money, and she'd give them time in the back room for a few minutes. Then she'd spend the rest of the day sleeping. My dad was a regular. Before he'd leave, he'd smile at me, stroke me on my cheek and say, "You know I'm your daddy, right?" I never responded.

Sometimes my mom would read to me. We had one book, a collection of poems from Edgar Allen Poe, her favorite author. There was a picture of the author on the back. She'd read to me, and I had no idea what she was talking about. But I liked that she would tell the story animated and she'd tickle me during the scary parts.

I remember when the social workers took me away. They called it a rescue, but I didn't think of it like that. My mom was all that I had ever known, and she was taken from me never to be seen again.

I don't remember much about my dad abusing me, but I remember pain. I remember my legs and my stomach hurting. I remember bleeding. I remember throwing up. The social worker noticed that I was walking funny so she took me to a hospital where they made me take off my clothes so they could examine me. I remember the doctor who took care of me. She was really nice. She talked calmly and slowly. She even gave me a teddy bear to help keep me calm during the exam.

When that was done, I got cleaned up and taken to a place where there were a lot of other kids. They were screaming, laughing, playing, and crying. It was noisier than anything I had ever encountered in my life. I missed my mom and the quiet of our apartment while she slept. I just held onto my bear and sat in a corner. I didn't want to talk to anyone. I was too afraid. Besides, who would understand how I felt? Who would understand what I was going through? All I wanted was my mother. All I wanted was for things to go back to normal.

As the months went on in that place, I knew that things would never be normal again and I started to get used to my new environment.

There was one kid there named Tony. He was goofy. He was always making silly noises and silly facial expressions. I smiled at him.

"Oh, there you go," one of our caretakers said to me. "Finally, a smile. You know you're cute when you smile. Well, cute for a Black girl."

I smiled harder. *I'm cute when I smile? Then I'll smile all the time.*

The agency had adoption parties monthly. Prospective parents would come and try to bond with all of us kids. I hated the parties because the other kids were louder and more obnoxious than usual. I was standing in a corner smiling during one of the parties when I saw this tall white man enter the building. He looked just like Edgar Allen Poe. He had brown hair, brown eyes, and a mustache. He walked stiffly looking as out of place as I felt. I followed him. It was the most familiar part of home that I had in that place of chaos.

I hoped he didn't notice as I stared. I didn't want him to see me. I just was curious to know what he was doing. But when he turned and looked at me, I had nowhere to hide. So, I did the only thing that I knew was cute, I smiled. He went about walking and I followed and smiled. Then he left and I was left wondering why Edgar Allen Poe was visiting such a chaotic place.

I soon found out when my social worker dropped me off at this mysterious man's house. She informed me that his name was William, not Edgar, and that he'd be my new foster dad and possibly my adopted dad if things went well.

His house was huge. I had never seen a house so big. It was a three-bedroom, two-and-a-half-bathroom house. The front yard was exquisitely decorated with grass, trees, and well-organized bushes. The closest neighbor had to be at least thirty feet from the house, not close enough to hear me scream. It was nothing like the one-bedroom apartment my mom and I shared in the heart of the hood. *What did one man need with all this space? And what did this man want with me? The only men I had known were the men who spent time with my mother and the one who hurt me.*

I found a corner, and I stayed planted until William enticed me with pizza. The pizza was good, best I'd ever tasted. And when I went to sit next to him, he didn't hurt me. He just talked and I listened pretending he was Edgar reading me more poems that I didn't understand.

It was quiet at William's house. Too quiet. No sounds of shouting, broken glass, or gunshots outside my window. No sounds of kids laughing or crying near my bed. I was afraid that night looking up at the shadows on the wall and nervously trying to figure out what object the shadow belonged to. I needed the reassurance that each shadow had an object and wasn't a demon trying to get me. Somehow, in the midst of all the shadow matching, I fell asleep.

I woke to the sounds of birds chirping and bacon sizzling on a stove. I held my teddy tight as I bravely ventured out of my room to see Edgar, I mean William, in sweatpants and a t-shirt slaving over the stove.

"Good morning, Chlo…Oh my God, your hair!" he said as he turned to look at me.

I touched my hair confused as to what he was talking about. My hair was still there and the texture was the same when I woke up in the morning without a good combing or brushing the night before. It was dry, thick and all over the place like usual.

"How do I do this?" William asked.

I shrugged and smiled.

"Yeah, Chloe, you're right. Let's eat first and worry about your hair later."

Bacon, eggs, potatoes, and pancakes were all new to me. I had never had a breakfast that large before. *Where was my stale sugary cereal?* I looked at the large meal before me and looked at William suspiciously. I didn't know where to start. I didn't know if I should eat it. I heard from Tony that White people couldn't cook and here was all this food in front of me. It smelled good but what if it was disgusting.

"Try it Chloe. It's good."

I started to cry.

"Uh oh. You don't like eggs and bacon," William tried to stay calm as he spoke.

"Well what do you like?"

I continued to cry.

"Oh, that's right, you don't talk. God, what to do? What to do?"

William got up and started running around the kitchen looking for something, anything that would keep me quiet. He was opening and closing the refrigerator and cabinets as if a miracle for my pain would miraculously appear in one of those areas.

"Milk, no. Chocolate, no not for breakfast remember boundaries. Chips, no. Huh, pizza! Yes. I mean it's not the healthiest for breakfast, but it worked last night."

He ran towards me with the cold pizza on a plate hoping it would be his saving grace.

I really didn't want the pizza either. But at least I knew it was good, so I took a bite.

"You know we can't eat pizza everyday Chloe." I smiled at him as I continued to chomp.

He smiled back and shook his head.

He went to grab a comb after I scarfed down my last bite. It was a cheap plastic comb he must have gotten from the dollar store. As soon as he touched the comb to my hair, it broke.

"Damn!" he fussed. "I mean darn it," he corrected himself when he saw my brown eyes peering at him. I smiled.

He ran to get a brush and started hacking and hawing at my hair as if he were trying to cut a path in a jungle with a machete. My scalp was on fire.

"Stop screaming...shhh...don't say a word," I remembered my birth father speaking to me as he covered my mouth and hurt me. I hated when flashbacks randomly invaded my thoughts. Sometimes it took me a few minutes to distinguish them from reality. With time they became less frequent but a year after my "rescue" they still occurred. I didn't say anything to William; I just started to cry. William continued to attack my hair not noticing my tears.

"Ha, high-ya," he said, "and a bow, perfect, yes. Okay, let's take a look in the mirror."

He ran and grabbed a mirror as I quickly wiped my tears away hoping that he wouldn't notice that I was crying again. He held the mirror up to my face revealing my new up-do. It looked like a bird's nest with a bow on top.

"Well, it's not perfect, but I tried my best. We've got to go, or else we'll be late for church."

Church? I had never been to church before. Never knew anyone who did go to church. I had flipped past a few sermons on TV at my old apartment on Sunday mornings when I was searching for cartoons, but I never listened to what they said. I wondered if it would be like the people on TV, yelling and fussing while people in the audience either nodded their heads or jumped around like they were having a seizure. It wasn't somewhere I was interested in going. I'd rather just stay in my corner. William ran around the room trying to get me and himself ready. He reminded me of Sonic the Hedgehog. I followed him with my eyes and smiled.

William handed me a cute little white dress and some uncomfortable shoes that he bought for me in anticipation of my arrival. I got dressed, grabbed Teddy, and followed William out to the car.

"Oh, the booster seat!" he remembered as he ran back into the house.

He struggled trying to get me safely and securely strapped into the car, "What the hell, oops, I mean heck…Okay, strap this here that there. I think I got it. Okay good."

He strapped me in tight and stood back proud of his accomplishment.

"Teddy's going to church too I see."

I smiled.

"Okay, just don't lose him."

We pulled up to a big building twenty minutes later. I could hear the music from the parking lot which was already filled with cars.

"Joy, joy, God's great joy!" I heard the choir singing as we approached.

"Brother William," a Black man greeted us at the door as he shook William's hand. I had never heard a Black man call a White man brother before. *What was he thinking? Was this a charade to get me to trust William? Why were we going to a Black church anyway? Was William trying to make me feel welcomed?*

"Mr. Thompson, so nice to see you? How's your family?"

"Oh fine, just fine. And who's this lovely lady?"

I clung to William's leg, the only familiarity in this strange place called church.

"This is Chloe, my uh, foster kid," he stumbled over what to call me.

"Hi Chloe, nice to meet you," Mr. Thompson bent down to shake my hand, but I did not want him to touch me. "You know we have a children's church. There's lots of kids your age there."

"What do you think Chloe?"

I wasn't sure what I wanted to do. I just wanted to get away from that strange man, so I tugged at William's jacket in attempt to get him to move on.

Chapter 3 – William's Autumn in 2007

I wasn't really sure if Chloe would feel more comfortable sitting with me in church or going to children's church. I asked, but all she did was smiled and tugged at my coat twice. I decided to walk to children's church with her and see if the two tugs meant that she wanted the second option instead of the first. The lady who greeted us at the door of children's church was a beautiful African American woman, someone who I had seen before in passing but never had the courage to introduce myself to. She had a caramel complexion with brown eyes and an hourglass figure. She had a nice inviting smile and she had long thick braids pulled up into a ponytail on the top of her head.

"Hi," she spoke. "Mr. Wilcox, right?"

I couldn't believe she knew my name. I shook my head, "yes." I was speechless as the sparkle in her eye made my heart skip a beat.

"And who do we have here," she said bending down to meet Chloe.

"This is Chloe, my foster daughter. I hope to one day adopt her officially."

"Well, hi Chloe. It's nice to meet you. From what I've heard, your dad has been a member of this church for several years. He seems like a pretty good guy huh."

Wow, this woman was wonderful. The word dad just rolled off her tongue naturally without force. It made me feel so special to be recognized as such. I had been crushing on this woman thinking she never saw me; but she did.

Chloe didn't respond. She just smiled.

"My name is Ms. Bianca. Would you like to come hang out with me and the other kids while your dad enjoys church service?"

Chloe nodded her head then grabbed Bianca's hand. Bianca stood up and whispered to me, "She's a beautiful girl. I'm guessing you didn't read the manual on Black hair though?"

"There's a manual?" I responded half joking. Bianca giggled.

"If you want, I could maybe come over one day and teach you how to do it. I have all boys, but I always wanted a girl so I could play in their hair."

"Yes!" I replied with a little too much enthusiasm. I adjusted my stance and forced myself to be more monotone, "Yes, that would be lovely."

"Okay then, I'll get your information after church service."

Church was beautiful and it offered the break I needed from fatherhood. Pastor spoke on the parable of the sower. "A sower went out to sow. And as he sowed, some seeds fell along the path, and the birds came and devoured them. Other seeds fell on rocky ground, where they did not have much soil, and immediately they sprang up, since they had no depth of soil, but when the sun rose, they were scorched. And since they had no root, they withered away. Other seeds fell among thorns, and the thorns grew up and choked them. Other seeds fell on good soil and produced grain, some a hundredfold, some sixty, some thirty. He who has ears, let him hear." He quoted Matthew 13:3-9. Pastor continued, "The soil represents our hearts. The seed represents God's word. How is your heart receiving God's word? Is your heart hard? Rejecting the word of God so that the Devil can easily come and snatch the word away before it even takes root in your heart. Is your heart shallow? It only accepts the word when life's conditions are good but as soon as troubles come your way you are willing to give up and reject God. Is your heart selfish? Easily influenced by the wealth, power, and temptations of this world which pierces and strangles the word that has been planted. Or is your heart willing to receive and keep the word of God?"

After church service I retrieved Chloe and got Bianca's information. Bianca worked as a secretary at a nearby high school. She agreed to come over after work the next day. I had already taken off two weeks of work in preparation for Chloe's arrival. I spent the entire next day cleaning and cooking making sure everything was perfect for when Bianca arrived. Chloe watched cartoons all day.

Bianca arrived punctually at 5 P.M, the time that we agreed on and she had her two little rambunctious boys with her. John was eight and James was ten. They had a lot of energy and from the time they came into the house they were busy tussling, talking, and bouncing off the walls. Bianca was firm with them but kind. Seemed like she had to correct them every 10 minutes. Chloe didn't seem fazed at all by the noise these two produced. She just sat there smiling.

"Okay," Bianca said as the boys settled in front of the TV. "So, how do you want Chloe's hair to be done?"

"Ummm, can you make it curly and out like it was when I first met her?"

"Sure! Curly hair, all you have to do is add water."

"Water?" I was confused, "Wait I thought water was a Black woman's kryptonite." I was joking but Bianca didn't laugh. I worried I had gone too far with the joke and offended her. She shook her head, brushed it off and proceeded to educate me on my ignorance.

"Well, if we straighten our hair, water will mess it up. But if you use water in the right way, it can be beneficial."

"Oh," I said having no clue what she was talking about.

Bianca got to work, "Let's see what type of hair you have Ms. Chloe."

She plucked a strand of Chloe's hair, retrieved a cup, filled it with water, and placed the strand of Chloe's hair into the water. She shook it around, picked up the strand, twirled, and pinched it with her fingers. "Ahhh, type 4A, this will be easy."

"4A?" I was riddled with awe as I watched Bianca perform her rituals.

"What kind of shampoo do you have?"

"Umm, I don't know."

"Don't you use shampoo?" Bianca questioned me.

"Yeah, I just use some generic stuff. Nothing special."

"No, generic stuff won't work for her. You will need sulfate free shampoo. Only wash her hair about once or twice a week in cool water and make sure you use a good conditioner after shampooing."

"Okay," I said trying to compute her language, "uh, should I be taking notes?"

She giggled, "If you want. Now, you want to use a light moisturizer every day. Something with coconut oil or olive oil should suffice."

Bianca filled a spray bottle with water and called Chloe over. She squirted the water onto Chloe's hair until it was saturated. Chloe just giggled and shrugged her shoulders. Bianca used her fingers to fluff out Chloe's hair then she tied it up with a pretty red ribbon. It was curly and beautiful again.

"Wow," I said. "It looks great."

Bianca smiled.

"Okay, so what do I do about tomorrow?"

Bianca giggled, "You know maybe I should come over next weekend and do some cornrows. They last longer. But as for tomorrow you can spray again and comb it out. Tonight, put some coconut oil on it then wrap it in a satin scarf."

"Got it. How much do I owe you?"

"Nothing," she answered.

"Really, you sure? At least let me pay for gas."

"I'm fine. We only live like fifteen minutes away."

I didn't have a satin scarf or coconut oil, so, I loaded Chloe in the car and made my way to the store.

I was completely lost staring in the ethnic hair aisle at Walmart. I picked up a scarf. "Is this what she was talking about?" I motioned to Chloe. Chloe tilted her head to the right. "No, I think that's cotton. We need satin." I found a pretty pink satin cap that I thought would work. I got a wide toothed comb, a firm brush, and every single hair oil that had the word olive or coconut on it. The shampoo was the hardest part. It seemed like everything I picked up had sulfate in it. I finally got to one brand that sported they were sulfate free. It cost fifteen bucks for the small size.

"Damn, fifteen bucks. Really?"

Chloe shrugged her shoulders.

"Your hair is expensive."

Chloe smiled.

"I think we are getting the hang of this communication thing, huh. Smile means yes, shrug means I don't know, and tilt means no. Cool. This could work."

Chloe smiled, took my hand, and started walking toward the door.

"Hold up Chloe, I've got to get a few more things."

We walked over to the food aisles where I picked up some eggs, pancake mix, and milk. As we walked past the frozen food aisle, Chloe opened up the freezer and took out two frozen pizzas.

"No Chloe, no more pizza for breakfast. We are having eggs tomorrow." I took the pizzas from her and put them back in the freezer.

Chloe tilted her head to the right and scrunched her eyebrows. Then she took the pizza back out of the freezer.

"Chloe, I said no." I attempted to grab the pizzas. She turned away from me and grunted. "Chloe, give me the pizza." She turned and grunted again. I grabbed her and grabbed the pizza. She threw her arms up in the air and let out a wail like I'd never heard before then she fell back on the ground and continued to wail and cry. Nosy people walked by slowly and gawked at me like I was trying to abduct her.

"Chloe get up," I whispered, "Get up." But my pleas fell on deaf ears as she continued the tantrum, and people continued their stares. I turned bright red and looked around panicking and wishing that some pleasant maternal soul would come rescue me. But no one helped, they all just stared in horror. I had to do something. So, I just picked Chloe up swung her over my shoulder and walked out of the store leaving the cart with all our supplies in the aisle. She screamed and kicked the whole way.

I strapped her in her booster seat and got into the driver's seat. She continued to wail. I sat in that parking lot with a wailing child in the back, and I just cried. I wasn't sure if I could be a dad. Maybe that's why God never blessed me with children of my own. Maybe He knew it wasn't for me. I was a failure. I had been in heated court rooms where freedom and lives were on the line but even that did not measure to the type of stress I was feeling at that moment.

"Just get home William. Just get home," I pumped myself up and wiped the tears away. I turned on the car and managed to drive. Halfway home, Chloe fell asleep. The much-desired silence gave me opportunity to hear from God, "William, I made you for this. I know it's hard, but this little girl needs you and you need her."

"If that's true, then Lord please give me strength and understanding cause I have no idea what I'm doing."

"Chloe has been through a lot. Just be patient. Things will work out."

I wanted to believe this was God's voice and not my own, but I wasn't sure. I had complete faith in God. But I had little faith in myself. When I reached home, I slowly and carefully unbuckled Chloe from her seat. I picked her up and carried her in the house. I walked slowly and smoothly like a teenager trying to sneak around. I didn't want to wake her and hear those wails again. If I could just get a few more hours to recuperate from our shopping spree, I'd be fine. I barely breathed as I tiptoed into her room and laid her down on her bed. I released her and slowly stood up while holding my breath. Then her eyes popped open.

I gasped in desperation hoping and praying that she would close her eyes and peacefully return to her nap. She didn't. She sat up in bed. I thought all hope was lost. But Chloe surprised me. She grabbed my arm and pulled me next to her. Then she rolled over onto her side and held my arm over her. I laid next to her, cuddling with her inhaling the fresh scent of her curly hair that was still tied up with a red ribbon and I fell asleep.

The crash of thunder woke me from my sleep around midnight. I looked down at Chloe who was still fast asleep and cozily wrapped in my arms. I gently removed my arm from her grasp and snuck out of her room.

"Okay God, I will stick with this. But you've got to help me out with this one," I prayed.

"You know I'll never leave you or forsake you," God responded.

**

But where was God now? My baby was laying in the ICU. Where was God? Where was He seven years ago when I got the call that changed my life forever? All the praying that I had done in my lifetime and when I really needed God to come through the most, He wasn't there. I was mad at God and I had held a grudge with Him for seven years. But I needed him. Maybe it was time to go back.

My thoughts were interrupted by the rushed entrance of Cadence, Chloe's best friend. Cadence was usually a wide-eyed bubbly girl, but her spark was replaced with genuine worry.

"Oh my God, I came as soon as I heard. Is she okay? Will she be okay? What happened? Can she hear me? Oh my God. I should have never left her alone at that…that…"

"At that what?"

"Nothing. Never mind."

"Are you sure about this Chloe?" I asked as I turned my white 2012 Ford Mustang onto North Gay Street. The neighborhood we drove through was unlike anything I had ever seen before. Half of the buildings were boarded up and condemned. There were several people walking the streets. Some were teenagers pushing strollers. Some were older men hunched over and falling asleep where they stood. Some were middle aged people with jeans and t-shirts scrambling like they were late for a job. They all carried the same facial expressions. Expressions of fatigue and hopelessness.

"Cadence, this may be my only chance to meet my mom."

We had skipped school that day and drove three hours from my safe haven of King George, Virginia to Baltimore, Maryland. Chloe was determined to find her birth mother. I didn't know why, but I chose to be supportive. With the help of a nerdy friend, Chloe was able to find her last known address. She held the piece of paper with the address scribbled on it tightly in her hand even though I had already programed our destination into my navigation system. I had never seen Chloe so excited before. She was usually so serious. But she sat in the passenger's seat with a big smile on her face as she looked out the window observing the hopeless people.

"In 500 feet make a left on unnamed road." I followed the car's command.

"You have reached your destination." My car's navigation landed us right in the middle of a scene from The Wire. There were raggedy old brown buildings all around and none of them said 3721 Clay Street on them. Few scraps of trash were blowing across the ground in the wind like tumbleweed from an old western movie. There were no kids playing. There were no moms pushing strollers. It was relatively quiet. There was a group of five tall Black men standing in a circle a few yards away from our car. They looked like football players in a huddle discussing their next move. They all had on black or blue jeans and white t-shirts. Their hair was in either cornrows, dreadlocks, or short knotty hair. As we pulled up, they all looked over towards us with suspicious defensive eyes. I don't think it helped that my windows were tinted, and the license plates were out of state.

"Maybe you should ask them for directions," I whispered to Chloe.

"I'm not asking them. You are the social butterfly. You do it."

"I'm not asking them. I don't want to die today. Could you imagine my cop-look-alike White ass approaching them? I'll end up on the news for sure. You're Black. They may warm up to you better."

"Doubt it. They don't know me. Besides, you know how to talk to people. Remember Johnnie?"

"Yeah, yeah, yeah," I stated as I reflected on the experience. It happened two years prior. It was the first time I experienced racism and privilege at its finest, though I didn't realize it at the time. After school one day, I had the bright idea to get snacks from Johnnie's store. I was craving some honey buns and the store was only five blocks away. Chloe was tired, she had stayed up the night before studying for an algebra test. She resisted the walk but ventured with me anyway. When we were almost at the store, my annoying older brother, Daniel, and his friends pulled up next to us and started threatening me with promises they would tell dad I was walking around being fresh. I motioned for a hot, exhausted, and annoyed Chloe to go into the store ahead of me while I argued with those idiots. Three minutes later, Chloe ran out of the store crying.

"What's wrong," I asked her. She proceeded to tell me that while she was shopping in the store, the owner approached her, accused her of shoplifting, and told her she was not allowed to come into the store anymore.

"Were you shoplifting?" I asked.

"No."

"Did you make some kind of gesture like put some items in your pocket that would make them think you were shoplifting even though you had the intention to pay for it?"

"No. I was carrying a bag of chips and a soda in my hand when he approached me."

"There must be some kind of mistake. Maybe Mr. Johnnie mistook you for someone else. Maybe you said something…"

"No!" Chloe yelled.

I could not make sense as to why she would be stopped and treated so badly. I figured there must have been some kind of misunderstanding. Maybe she said the wrong words. Maybe her tired expressions looked angry or suspicious to Mr. Johnnie. I didn't realize that racism still existed in America. We had a Black president. My dad always taught me that racism was a thing of the past. He explained Black people had the same opportunities that we all had but they didn't advance because they didn't pursue their opportunities.

"Well maybe I should go and talk to him," I grabbed a very resistant Chloe by the wrist and marched into the store.

"Mr. Johnnie, my friend and I would like to purchase two bags of chips, a honey bun, and two Sprites. Is that okay with you?"

"Yes, ma'am," Johnnie expressed respectfully. He showed us where the snacks were and rang them right up.

"See," I naively said to Chloe when we left the store. "Sometimes you just have to know how to talk to people."

She rolled her eyes but didn't educate me. Later, I discovered just how unfair life was for her. Nevertheless, Chloe never let me forget my past ignorance. She mentioned it every now and then, but it was more of an inside joke than an insult.

I whispered a prayer, "Lord please be with me," as I rolled down the window. I decided to put on my sweet innocent damsel in distress voice, "Umm, excuse me sir. I am so lost. Could you please help me and my friend?"

The aggressive facial expressions changed when they realized we weren't a threat. One of the guys smiled at us revealing a full front row of gold teeth. "Sure Shorty," he replied, "where you headed?"

"Oh, umm we are trying to find 3721 Clay street apartment A."

"Oh, yeah! That's right across the yard," he said as he motioned to a sidewalk that went through a courtyard to another brown building. "You can park right here. We'll make sure no one messes with you."

"Super! Thank you so much. I really appreciate you helping us out." I parked the car, and I whispered to Chloe, "Good ole damsel in distress routine. It works every time. Doesn't matter if you are a middle aged professional or a young thug. All men fall for it." Then I winked at her. Chloe's excitement had changed to worry as she reluctantly got out of the car. "Well, don't get scared now. We are here. No need to worry. Chloe and Cadence against the world remember?" I held out my pinky finger.

"Chloe and Cadence." She sighed and entangled her pinky finger around mine. Then we both exited the car.

"Y'all not from 'round here huh!" We both shook our head no. "Who y 'all lookin' for?"

"Maybeline Price?" I asked more than stated.

"Maybeline…Maybeline… Aye yo Spike, you know a Maybeline?"

"Naw" responded a boy who couldn't have been older than twelve. He was sitting on a crate several yards away.

"Spike know e'ryone. Maybeline got a nickname or sompin'?"

"We don't know. She's my mother. I think." Chloe responded.

"Oh," he said in a way that made me think he knew exactly what Chloe was going through. "Well if your mama from dees parts, dat means you family. My name's Lil Man. That's Squad, Smoke, Blaze, and Chuck," They each gave a head nod as Lil Man called their names. "And ya'll know Spike o'er there." Spike threw up a deuce sign as he was introduced. "Come on, I'll walk you o'er there"

We followed him across the courtyard to the apartment. He stood outside as we walked up the broken concrete steps and down the hallway of the building to apartment A. We knocked on the door and waited. No answer. We knocked again. No answer. But from apartment B we heard the sounds of chains unlashing and locks opening. The door inched open just enough to reveal one eyeball peering out at us.

"Who ya lookin' fo?" an elderly lady's voice rang from inside the apartment.

"Umm, Maybeline Price," I said.

"Don't know no Maybeline. Know a Leena though. She lived there 'bout 3 years ago before she..." The lady stopped midsentence as she looked closer at Chloe. She stepped out of her apartment slowly, "Chloe, Little Chloe Price, that's you ain't it."

"Yes, I'm Chloe. Chloe Wilcox now."

"Oh, you got married," the elderly woman said as she smiled with genuine care and pride.

"No ma'am; not married. Adopted."

"Ohhh, well your mother…huh, your mother…" Her face turned from excited to concerned. "Girls, come on in here, let me make you some tea." I looked back at Lil Man who gave me a head nod when he saw we were in good hands then made his way back to the huddle. We followed her into her apartment. It was a dimly lit place only illuminated by a small lamp that sat on the opposite side of a plastic wrapped couch. There was an old TV that still had an antenna and dials sitting on top of a wooden coffee table at the far end of the room. It was simple and neat.

"Have a seat. I'm Ms. Tina. You used to call me Aunt T when you were little. Chloe, you remember that?" Chloe shook her head no as Ms. Tina prepared tea using a tea pot and a stove, the old-fashioned way. "I reckon you wouldn't. That was oh, what 12-13 years ago? You and your mama stayed right next to me in apartment A. Your mama was a kind woman. She loved you dearly. You were her pride and joy. She'd die for you and almost did, you know. When she found out Ole' Willie was puttin' his hands on you. She flipped out. She ain't care that she was half his size nor that he ran with the biggest gangsters in the east side. As soon as he got out of jail, she went to whoopin' on his ass in the middle of the courtyard where everybody was a witness. Man, he threatened to kill her but she ain't care. She said 'try and I'll fuck you up again.' Woo, it was hilarious. After that people started calling him Whimpy instead of Willie and that name stuck till his death in 2014."

"Willie? That was my father. How'd he die?"

"Willie claimed he was your father but truthfully, no one really know'd who ya real daddy was. Leena dated Willie when she was 'bout five months pregnant with you and already showin'. Anyway, he was shot. That's how he died. No one knows who shot him. He was a dealer so probably a rival dealer or sompin' like dat."

"And my mom, what happened to her?"

"Oh, Leena…" Miss Tina spoke with sadness. "Leena had a problem with drugs ya know. When she lost you, her drug problem got worse. About three years ago she overdosed. Was found dead in her apartment a few days after she died. Beat myself up pretty bad about it. It was me who called child protective services for ya. I was hoping they'd just arrest Willie. Didn't think they'd take you away from your mama too. I am so sorry."

Chloe didn't respond. She just looked down at the floor. I wrapped my arm around her. The tea pot began to whistle.

"Tea's ready. Y'all want some?"

"No thanks," Chloe responded.

"I think we should probably get going. We've got a long drive ahead of us."

Ms. Tina nodded and walked us to the door. "Oh, Chloe, hold up. If you ever need anything or have any questions about your ma. Please don't hesitate to call." She quickly scribbled her number on a piece of paper and handed it to Chloe. Chloe's face remained stoic as she took the number and put it in her pocket.

The car ride home was quiet. Chloe didn't say a word the entire three hours. She blankly stared out the window. I didn't know what to say so I kept quiet. Often, in between gear shifts I'd take her hand in mine and caress it. She didn't move at my touch. I was worried about her. And over the next few weeks I made sure to keep a close eye on her. I called her twice a day, but she never really wanted to talk. At school I followed her around despite her trying to reassure me that she was okay. She didn't look okay. She looked depressed. On the weekends I came over usually bringing her favorite foods, pizza, chocolate chip cookie dough ice cream, and Takis. She never had an appetite.

My friend fell into a deep depression and I was scared for her. It took all the energy I had to put a little glimpse of a smile on her face. I wanted to tell someone that I was worried for my friend and why. But I knew if I did, we would both get our asses handed to us for skipping school and venturing around the projects. She would never forgive me. So, I kept quiet and continued to muster up the strength to keep her afloat.

**

It was my idea to go to Jeremy's party. I figured it would cheer her up. I didn't think she'd overdose on drugs when we went. She never messed with drugs before. But I was so engulfed with the attention I received from the captain of the basketball team that I forgot all about my friend's woes. When I asked her if it was okay that I dipped out, she seemed fine. I should have never left her.

It was only a few hours later that I got a text from Jeremy letting me know that Chloe was in the hospital. I rushed to her side as soon as I heard and was faced with Mr. Wilcox's questions.

Chapter 5 – Chloe's Autumn in 2014

It was my first day of high school. New town, new house, new school, and I was beyond nervous. Dad dropped me off at the entrance even though I suggested he stop a couple of blocks away.

"Bye honey! I love you!" he loudly spoke then waited for my response.

"Love you too," I quickly mentioned through clenched teeth then hurried up the steps. As I entered, I observed all the hustle and bustle of teenagers talking loudly and moving seemingly with ease through the crowded hallways. They all looked comfortable in their own bodies, which was completely contradictory to the extreme awkwardness I felt. I felt out of place and uncomfortable like I was wearing someone else's clothes. I searched the crowd trying to find a friendly face that looked lost too. I planned on introducing myself to whoever that person was and maybe we could be lost together. But all the faces I saw had carefree smiles as they greeted old friends and caught up on last summer's events. The cliques were already formed, and I did not seem to fit in any of them. I looked down at my schedule. My homeroom was room number 3G2B.

"Umm excuse me can you tell..." the rambunctious boy breezed by completely ignoring my attempt to ask for directions. "Excuse me can you..." a girl this time, also ignored me and instead laughed with her small group of friends.

Then the bell rang signifying that we should be sitting in our first class. It seemed like the halls emptied immediately leaving me alone and lost in the main hallway. I wandered aimlessly until spotting hallway 3G and making my way to the door marked 3G2B. The door was locked, and an annoyed looking teacher made her way to answer it while she continued to address the rest of the class without mentioning my tardiness. I spotted an empty seat in the front center which I quietly moved to occupy. But a gust of wind rushed past me from the door and occupied the seat instead. She was a spunky blonde-haired little thing. She smiled brightly after she sat in the seat and seemed to be oblivious to her own indiscretions.

The teacher noticed my frustration. "There's a seat in the back Miss uh what is your name?"

"Chloe."

"Oh yes, Chloe. Well nice to meet you. Go take your seat. You get a pass this time, but please ensure that you are not late to my class again." I sat in the back of the class using my anger filled eyes to burn a hole in the back of that blondie's neck. I barely paid attention to the teacher overviewing the curriculum for the year.

"And we will be talking about the American Civil War, slavery, and the Civil Rights Movement in the month of February…Chloe I am sure you will find that month particularly interesting," the teacher broke my concentration.

"Huh, oh yes ma'am!" I responded but I couldn't help to wonder why she singled me out for that topic. I looked around the classroom – white face, white face, white face. I realized quickly that I was the only person of color in the classroom. The bell rang. I quickly grabbed my books and headed for the door. I didn't want to be late to my second class as well. When I got into the hallway. There was a white face, white face, and another white face. Was I the only Black person in school? I raced toward my next class looking along the way for anything different, Spanish, Asian, Indian, African, or Native American. There was nothing but white faces everywhere I looked.

When I walked into my next class, I was so happy to see one Asian girl who sat in the middle of the room. "Hi!" I spoke taking a seat next to her. She rolled her eyes, flipped her hair, and spoke to a White girl that was sitting on the other side of her. *Oh boy, this is going to be a long school year,* I thought. I attended two more classes, and no one spoke to me. Then it was lunch. I stood in the middle of the cafeteria looking for an inviting face to sit with but there was none. There was an empty table near the trash cans. I figured that would be my best bet. I sat there and ate.

"Hi!" the same blonde-haired girl that stole my seat at first period spoke as she stood over me. I rolled my eyes. It was instinctive. I didn't mean to be so rude to the only person in the entire school that acknowledged my existence. I straightened my face and responded, "Hi. Would you like to sit down?"

"Yes! Thank you so much. My family just moved here from North Carolina. I am so lost in this school. It's much bigger than the school I'm used to. It's so good to see a friendly face. It's so nice to meet you. I'm Cadence! What's your name?" she extended her hand to greet me. Her blue eyes were big and bright like they were ready to take in the entire world. Every word she spoke was bubbly and chipper.

"I'm Chloe. It's nice to meet you."

"First day of high school! Isn't it exciting! I can't believe I'm a freshman, can you? I can't wait for homecoming and, oh my God, prom…" and Cadence went on and on. I don't think she took a breath or ate a bite of food. I just sat their partially listening, partially eating, but mostly wondering, *who is this creature and why is she so happy?* "…my favorite color is rainbow, and my spirit animal is a unicorn. What's yours?"

"Huh," I asked.

"Um, spirit animal. You know the animal whose personality you most connect with. Mine is a unicorn or at least that's what my mom always said. Though I have no clue why. Unicorns don't exist. But my mom said they were magical, just like me! I don't see it."

I did. I noticed Cadence's very magical personality with our first conversation. I knew right then and there we'd be great friends. Cadence took out the first item from her lunchbox, Cheetos. Then she took out some chopsticks. She opened the Cheetos and used her chopsticks to eat them.

"What are you doing?" I asked.

"Oh, I always eat Cheetos with chopsticks. That way my fingers don't get all cheesy."

I realized that Cadence was not only bubbly and magical. She was also a genius.

"Never thought of that. Smart!"

"Yeah, I learned it from my mom. She's dead now."

"Your mom? Wow sorry to hear that,"

"Oh, no worries. She's been gone for several years now. I've got my dad, and my brother still so I'm good. So, what is your spirit animal?"

"I don't know. I never thought about it. Um, a sloth?"

Cadence laughed. "No, I don't see that at all. I see an elephant! Quiet, fierce, and strong but with a really sweet, humble, and kind heart. Yep, that's you!"

She was right though I didn't know it at the time. "Wait, your favorite color is rainbow? How is that possible? You can only have one favorite color," I stated realizing what she said previously. She was talking quickly, and my brain wasn't catching things until a few sentences later.

"Not me, I like all the colors. Though I wish that the LGTBQ didn't use that as their symbol. Kind of messes up my flow, you know?"

"No?"

"Well, I want to have rainbows all over the place-on my shoes, in my room, on my book bag. But my dad prohibits it. He is excessively big into church. He doesn't want me having the gay symbol on all my stuff you know. Does your family go to church?"

"No, we used to but my dad he stopped going."

"Oh, sorry to hear that." The bell rang. "Well, got to go! See you later!"

My favorite part of school became first period and lunch because those were the times I got to hang out with the magical Ms. Cadence. Over the next few weeks our lunch crew grew to a whopping three. Joshua, who we lovingly called Joshie, was a nerdy math genius that I met in gym class. He usually spent his lunch doing his homework. When he didn't have homework, he'd do practice math problems, for fun. He didn't talk much but he was good company. He was always willing to help Cadence and I if we had questions about any of our classes.

The cafeteria was segregated into various clicks. The jocks sat together, the gorgeous fashionistas sat together, the nerdy gamers sat together, and the ambitious future CEOs sat together. Then there was us. I enjoyed my company, all of us unique and awkward. But my attention continuously veered over to the jock table where Michael Harris sat with his fellow lacrosse players.

Michael was a sophomore and the most handsome guy I had ever laid eyes on. He was 6'4" with dark hair, dark eyes, and a flawless complexion. His teeth were perfectly straight, and I swear they sparkled when he smiled. At, fifteen he had huge biceps and a six pack. His Instagram was filled with pictures of him flexing while shirtless. I was a dedicated follower. He never noticed me. But his freshman friend Jeremy noticed Cadence. Often Jeremy would stop by our table on the way to his own to make small talk. There was no depth to our conversations. Just a simple "Hey, how you doing? Nice weather we're having" dialogue. Jeremy was cute but Cadence obviously was not interested. She said she wanted someone with more depth. That never stopped Jeremy from trying.

**

My dad was super protective of me. He had a busy life, but it didn't stop him from dropping me off and picking me up from school every day. I volunteered to ride the bus, but he didn't want me coming home to an empty house. I'd start on my homework as I waited on the steps at the front of school for him to pick me up. Often, he was late. He'd be stuck in a court case that went on longer than expected. Many times, he would have to drop me off at the house then return to his chambers to brush up on a few things. His dedication to giving me a ride was pointless. Nevertheless, he insisted.

"Hey, what are you still doing here?" Cadence's voice interrupted my after-school study session one day.

"Waiting for my dad. What about you?"

"Waiting for my brother, Daniel. He has basketball practice today. Start of the season, you know how that goes." Daniel was a junior at our school. He had his own car and gave Cadence a ride to and from school. When basketball wasn't in season, they left promptly. But during season, Cadence had to wait around for her brother to finish practice before she could get home. Despite Daniel being a new kid in school, he quickly rose to become one of the most popular. His basketball skills were the likely cause of his rapid rise to the top of the high school food chain. Whoever said, "White men can't jump," never met Daniel Ellison. He was the most talented ball player that King George County had ever seen. Dunks, lay-ups, free throws – everything that Daniel shot miraculously made it in the hoop. Cadence found him annoying. They had a typical brother-sister love-hate let's try our best to get on each other's nerves type of relationship. But if one of them was hurting, the other would lay down their life to help.

My dad pulled up and at the sight of me talking with someone, he quickly jumped out of the car to meet her. He had been pressing me to make new friends since before school even started. And he wanted to get to know each and every friend I met.

"Hi Chloe! Who's your friend?" You could see the excitement in his face.

"Dad this is Cadence. Cadence this is my dad." Usually when people see my dad and me together, they blink a couple of times and look sideways in attempt to figure out how we are related. But not Cadence. She didn't even notice our race discrepancy. She was completely color blind and she didn't miss a beat.

"Hi Mr. Wilcox! It is so nice to meet you. I usually eat lunch with Chloe. She is a good friend."

"Well, it is nice to meet you too Cadence. Do you need a ride?"

"Oh no thank you. I am waiting for my brother. He should be done with practice soon."

"Oh, okay well you have a nice day. Take care." Dad put his arm around me and walked me to the car. "She seems nice," he whispered to me.

"She is. The nicest." I smiled.

Chapter 6 – James' Frost in 2018

I walked back to my dorm room pissed. I couldn't believe I got a D on that organic chemistry test. I stayed up all night studying for it. There was no way I'd get into graduate school with those kinds of grades. It was my fourth year in college, and I had no idea what I was going to do next. I racked up seventy-five thousand dollars in school loans and if I were not going to graduate school, I'd have to find a job promptly to be able to start paying that debt back. But there were no jobs for a Black man who only had a bachelor's degree in biology.

My cell phone vibrated in my pocket. "Hello," I answered without looking at the number.

"James, its Chloe. She's in the hospital," William's voice said in a worried tone.

"What!? What's wrong!? Is she okay?"

"No. It's serious. It's bad."

"I'm on my way."

"You don't have to come all the way over here. I just wanted to let you know what was going on and ask for your prayers."

"Mr. William, I'm coming right away. See you tonight."

I ran to my dorm room, packed a bag, and raced up I-95 until I got to Spotsy Regional Hospital.

"Only immediate family is allowed in the ICU," the nurse at the information desk said.

"Yes, I'm her brother."

The nurse looked at me like I had three heads, "Hold on." She picked up a phone and dialed a number. "Yes, I have a visitor for Chloe Wilcox...He says he is her brother...No this one is Black...okay, I'll hold." We stood in uncomfortable silence as she waited for the person on the other end to respond. "He said that's his son too...okay!"

The nurse scribbled the words ICU 3 on a tag and handed it to me, "Here, you'll need this. She is only allowed two visitors at a time so your other sister will have to come out before you can go in."

Other sister? I wondered who she was talking about. Growing up it had just been Chloe, John, and I. There were no other sisters. But I went with it. As I walked into the ICU, a White girl with tears in her eyes walked out. She half smiled at me as I passed her as if she knew who I was, but I had never seen her before.

William sat next to Chloe's bed holding her hand. His face was red and puffy. I could tell he had been up all-night crying. I hadn't seen or spoken to him in seven years, but he still looked the same. I remember being so angry at him all those years ago. But looking at him that day, how broken he appeared, I had no grudge in my heart, only love and sympathy.

"James!" He stood as he saw me.

"Mr. William," I replied trying to maintain distance. But I couldn't help to feel close to him that day. He reached out to me and gave me exactly what I needed, a big hug. I melted in his arms. That display of empathy was something that I craved from him for a long time. Previously, he was emotionally unavailable and as a result I withdrew. But with Chloe in critical condition, we needed each other's support.

Chloe was not my biological sister but from the day I met her she had been a sister to me. I loved her dearly. And even though I stopped talking to William, I still talked to Chloe at least once a week. She wasn't the type to take drugs or drink so when William told me why she was in the ICU, I was unbelieving and looking for other answers.

"Did they find out what happened?" I asked.

"No they are still running tests."

"You don't really think she did drugs, do you? That's not Chloe's character."

"I don't know. You know her biological mom was a druggy. There is a genetic component to addiction. And she's been acting, well, not herself lately."

"There's got to be another explanation. Hey, who was that girl I saw walking out of the ICU?"

"That's Cadence. She's Chloe's best friend. She was with her the night this happened."

"Mmmm, looks like me and Cadence gonna have to have a little talk."

"I'm sure she'll be back. Right now, spend some time with Chloe. She's always respected you so talk to her. The nurse said she can hear our voice. I'm going to go get some coffee."

I refused to shed a tear while William was there but after he left, I cried like a baby and prayed like a saint though I was neither. I told Chloe how much I loved her, and I encouraged her to fight for her life. I squeezed her hand, but it remained lifeless. I sat there staring at her hand and remembering how I felt the last time I was in a hospital. It was a memory that randomly invaded my thoughts. I didn't expect it to come that day; but it did, and I had about all I could take of ICU room 3. I had to go get some fresh air.

I walked back out to the waiting room where I saw Cadence and some nerdy looking guy.

"You're Cadence, right?"

"Yes, and you're James. Chloe talks about you all the time."

"Yes, and who are you?" I pointed to the nerd.

"I'm Joshua. I'm a friend."

"Were you there the night this happened too?"

"Yes," Joshua said as he adjusted his glasses and shifted his stance. Cadence looked sincerely innocent. But Joshua looked guilty as sin, and he was about to get the third degree from me.

I stepped closer to him, "So what happened?"

"Umm, I'm not sure. She was drinking a lot and…um…that's all I know," he stuttered, that was a red flag to me. He was hiding something.

"Joshie," Cadence interrupted, "Show him."

Joshua side-eyed her in protest.

"Go ahead, maybe he can help us figure out what happened."

Joshua rolled his eyes. "Fine," he said as he took out his phone and showed a video that he had received in a text message from an unknown number.

The video was mainly of people partying and getting drunk; but in the periphery, there was Chloe arguing with a tall White boy. She didn't look drunk. She looked angry and hurt. He grabbed her arm with his left hand, grabbed a beer with his right, and marched her off into a room slamming the door behind them.

"Who was that?"

"Michael Harris," Cadence answered. "He graduated from our high school last year. He is supposed to be away at college. I have no idea what he's doing back here."

"Do you know what they were arguing about?"

"Not a clue. He and Chloe didn't even hang out like that. I tried to call him. He won't answer."

"You know where he lives?"

Cadence shook her head no.

"I do," Joshua chimed in.

"You're taking me to him now."

"I'm driving," Cadence whipped out her keys. She was just as ready as I was to find answers.

We pulled into Michael's driveway, got out, and rang the bell. A middle age balding White man with a beer belly answered. It was 3 P.M on a Monday and this man was already shit-faced. Alcohol was dripping out of his pores. He held a half empty bottle of vodka in his hand.

He looked hard at Cadence and Joshua but looked harder at me. "What you want?"

"Is Michael here?"

"Who wants to know?"

"I'm Cadence, this is Joshua, and James. We are friends of Chloe and..."

"Chloe? Chloe Wilcox? That Black bitch done already ruined his life! What more do you want? Get off my property before I call the police on ya!"

"But sir..." Cadence couldn't get the rest of her sentence out before the door was slammed in her face. I was upset before, but I was furious after that encounter. Michael did something to my sister and his racist alcoholic father was covering it up. I went back to the hospital where I immediately requested the nurses do a rape kit on Chloe. William initially was in protest but after a second, he realized I was right, and he too insisted it be done.

Chapter 7 – Bianca's Seasons

I first met Chloe and William a few months after my divorce from Nathaniel was finalized. I knew William wanted more than a friendship with me. But I was not ready to open up my heart to him or anyone for that matter. My ex-husband scarred me. He was physically and mentally abusive. I put up with nine years of punches, slaps, kicks, hair pulls, and choking. I had been called worthless, ugly, and stupid so many times I eventually started to believe it. I had contemplated leaving for all nine years. But I didn't have a solid way out. I had two sons, no job, no friends, and my family hadn't talked to me since I got pregnant at the age of sixteen. Nathaniel told me he would kill me and my boys if I left and I believed him. Once he caught me when I tried to pack my bags and escape. He held a gun to my head and told me he would pull the trigger unless I got on my knees and begged him to take me back. I did and I waited years before attempting another escape. When Nathaniel first put his hands on my youngest son, John, I decided to step out on faith. John was only six and after the beating he had bruises from his neck to his toes.

While Nathaniel was at work, my sons and I left only with what we could carry, and we checked into a woman's shelter. They had several resources. Lawyers who took on clients pro bono, assistance with getting a restraining order, job fairs, and a place for me and my babies to lay our heads. It wasn't the fanciest of places, but it was a step to independence.

It took a while to get a lawyer, the resources were limited, but eventually I did, and after two years of court appearances the divorce was finalized. In the divorce decree Nathaniel was ordered to pay 400 dollars a month in child support, and it was supposed to get garnished from his check. On the way out of the courtroom he approached me and stated, "You'll never get a dime."

That was the first time in all my years of knowing him that he kept his promise. He quit his job to avoid garnishment, and I stopped hearing from him. That was fine with me. I didn't want him around to beat up on my boys or influence them. I was reluctant to fight further for child support because I feared he would retaliate with violence. My life was quiet and peaceful. Though poor, I was content.

I got a job as a secretary and saved up enough money for me and my boys to move out of the shelter into a one-bedroom apartment. The apartment was across the street from a church. On Sunday mornings I would hear the calls of gospel songs radiating. One morning, I got my boys dressed and walked in. My life was forever changed. Immediately, my heart was full. You know that feeling you get when you first fall in love. Like your heart has been stuffed with butterflies and is about to explode. It felt like that only stronger and purer. I thought I found love at sixteen but that was counterfeit love. What I felt in the church was genuine. It was something I longed for most of my life. I never thought that walking into a church would be the answer, but it was. Immediately I fell on my face and wailed like a baby. My boys stood staring at me not sure whether to be happy or afraid. A few people in the church came to their rescue, and mine. William was one of the rescuers. He comforted my boys while I continued to be overwhelmingly filled with the Holy Spirit. Women of the church covered me with sheets and prayed while I cried.

I joined church and gave my life over to God that day. I started going to both Sunday services, Tuesday Bible study, and Saturday morning prayer. I feared my boys would feel rejected because I spent so much time with Jesus. I decided to get them more involved as well. I signed them both up for children's choir, and I volunteered for children's church for the second service. That way I could listen to the sermon in the mornings and serve while spending time with my kids in the afternoon. A few months later, William spoke to me for the first time when he walked in with his adopted daughter.

Initially Chloe only talked to my sons James and John. They had a special bond. Whenever William and I would come into the room, she'd immediately clam up and smile at us. But when we stepped out and listened at the door, we could hear her yapping away. It took a year and a half, but gradually she opened up to William and me. She talked a lot about William. It was obvious she was appreciative of him adopting her and treating her with kindness. That's when I knew I could trust William and after a while, I let my guard down.

William was always worried about me. "What kind of man doesn't want to raise his kids?" he'd ask. "You guys shouldn't be living like this," he'd mention. I wished he would let it go but he pressed it. He insisted representing me at no charge. He said it was payback for doing Chloe's hair so many times. I resisted but eventually he wore me down. Then William became even more driven. He spent hours tracking Nathaniel down and having him served for court. In court, William was well prepared. He had Nathaniel's pay stubs, bank account statements, asset values, tax documents, and loans prepared and organized. He was able to prove that Nathaniel should be paying and could afford to pay 800 dollars a month plus back-pay for unpaid child support.

It took a few court dates but, in the end, the judge ruled in my favor. Nathaniel was ordered to pay 800 dollars a month plus $21,000 in back pay and court fees. All would be garnished from his check, bank account, and tax refund check. Nathaniel was threatened with license suspension if he didn't comply.

I jumped for joy when I got the first check in the mail. In combination with my income and savings, it was enough to move from a one-bedroom apartment to a three-bedroom condominium. William and Chloe helped us move.

"Where's the bathroom?" Chloe whispered to James as soon as we arrived at the new place. James wasn't sure. That day was his first day in the new place as well.

"First door on the right," I said. Chloe scurried off. Seconds later I heard a gut-wrenching cry from the bathroom. William ran to the door, "Chloe! You okay?"

"I'm dying!" she cried.

"What do you mean you're dying?" he tried to open the door, but it was locked. "Chloe, unlock the door. What's wrong baby?"

The bathroom door clicked open. William rushed in first with his fists up looking like he was going to fight whoever was trying to hurt his Chloe. I came in second just trying to figure out what the fuss was about. Then I saw it, blood in the toilet. Chloe was huddled in a corner crying. She was nine years old and probably had no idea what was happening to her.

"Chloe, honey," I said as I bent down to hold her. "It's your period. Oh, baby, it's okay." I rocked her.

"Her period! Oh God no! This can't be happening. She's too young," William overdramatically reacted.

"Oh my God!" Chloe matched his fear, "I don't want to die! I'm too young," she wailed.

"William, grab the boys and get out," I demanded. "Let Chloe and I have girl talk."

"Umm, okay…okay, boys come on. There's nothing to see here," he ushered James and John who were curiously trying to see what was going on.

"Chloe," I said to her in a gentle tone when we were alone. "You are not going to die. This is something that naturally happens to women."

"They bleed?"

"Yes baby. Once a month you will bleed from your vagina. It's our body's way of cleaning itself."

Chloe knew nothing about puberty, her body, or sex. We sat there for a good hour talking about everything this nine-year-old menstruating girl could handle. Enough to keep her clean, safe, and out of trouble. In the end she gave me a hug and said, "Thanks Ms. Bianca. I don't remember my mom very well, but I'm glad God gave me you." And the butterflies once again ravished my heart.

"Is she okay?" James asked as we exited the bathroom. He was always my little protector. He tried to protect John and me from Nathaniel all those years and from the time when he first met Chloe, he kept a watchful eye on her too.

"She's okay worry-wart," I responded as I playfully punched him in the arm. "Go play!" I encouraged them to go in the room and play together.

"Thank you for that," William whispered as I positioned myself next to him in the kitchen. "I don't know what I would have done without you."

"No worries. You know Chloe's young but she's smart. I think she can…" William kissed me in the middle of my sentence. I looked at him stunned. He looked just as stunned. Words tried to form in his mouth, but he couldn't get them out. I leaned over and kissed him back. I felt his body relax as our kiss continued. I wrapped my arms around his neck. He grabbed my waist and pulled me close to him. I could feel his heart racing against my own. His lips were soft against mine. Passion warmed my body.

"I wanted to do that for a long time," he said.

I smiled. "Oh yeah? How long?"

"Since the first day you walked into church. I think I fell in love with you that day."

I giggled. "You remember that?"

"Yes, you unapologetically wailed. I could tell by your cry you had been through a lot. But I could also tell that you're a survivor. Your spirit is pure, and your heart is genuinely good."

"You figured out all that the first time you saw me?"

"Yes, I felt connected to you spiritually. And the more I got to know you, the more I realized my initial assessment was correct."

"So, you're saying you're in love with me."

"Yes!"

"Well, William I love you too." His smile reached from ear to ear then he pulled me closer and kissed me deeply. That was the beginning of the best relationship I'd ever been in. The love that William showed for my boys and I was something I never experienced from another person before. He catered to my needs. If I needed some space, he'd take the boys and give me a few hours to myself. If I needed to be held, he'd hold me all night. If I was hungry and tired, he'd hand me the remote, tell me to relax and allow me to watch TV while he cooked a delicious meal. If my feet hurt after a long day, he'd massage them. And I did the same for him. We spent many of nights talking, laughing, and enjoying each other's company. We had completely different backgrounds, and he was eleven years my senior, but it was our differences that made us strong. We could relate, respectfully disagree, and learn from each other.

It went on like that for several months, then one Saturday morning I was woken by a loud knock on my door. I ignored it at first, pulling the covers over my head then I heard the knock again. I dragged myself out of bed and looked through the peephole. I prayed to God it wasn't Nathaniel. He had been blowing up my phone with crude text messages which I always ignored. There were a few times he'd stop by drunk demanding to see the boys. I had been successful in fending him off without getting William or the police involved. Luckily, it was William and Chloe's smiling faces shining at me through the hole. I was too tired to get excited. I opened the door.

"Good morning sunshine!" he said when he saw me. I crawled to the couch and planted my face in the cushions.

"William what are you doing? It's seven A.M on a Saturday. Don't you sleep?" William and I had been up until one A.M talking on the phone. I was baffled about how he could be up, dressed, and at my door with Chloe just six hours later.

"I couldn't sleep. I was too excited," he said as he put his arms around me and laid with me on the couch. He kissed all over my face.

"I've got morning breath." I tried to shield my face from his kisses.

"I love your stinky breath."

I laughed and kissed him back.

"Okay, okay," Chloe said. "Come on, it's time to get up. You're going to be late."

"Late?" I asked.

"Yes, Bianca. Today is your day, and I have planned something incredibly special for you," William cheerfully spoke as he stood up and took my hand.

"What?"

"Yep! I'm taking the boys and you're going…" he handed me a card with an address and my keys.

"Okaaaaay?"

"Hurry get dressed. You've got thirty minutes."

I had a million questions, but I figured I'd just go with whatever crazy scheme William had planned. I brushed my teeth. "What should I wear?" I yelled from the bathroom.

"Something casual and comfortable. Oh, and you'll need sandals."

Sandals? Was he planning to take us to the beach?

"Sandals or flip flops?" I asked knowing that men often didn't realize the difference.

"It doesn't matter," William hollered back.

I sighed and rolled my eyes. I decided to play it safe and put on a casual sundress and some flip flops.

"Go, go, go," William ushered me out of the door. "You've got fifteen minutes."

I formed my mouth to ask more questions; but I saw Chloe's smiling face staring at me, and I knew everything was going to be alright. I went and drove to the address on the card. 667 Pitt Street. I pulled up to a quaint hair salon. I walked in.

"Ms. Bianca?" a nice lady greeted me at the door.

"Yes, that's me."

"I'm Karen. I'll be handling your hair today."

"Okay?" I had questions but I reminded myself that I'd go with the flow and I did. Karen hooked my hair up. She washed, deep conditioned, trimmed, and styled it in an adorable natural up-do.

"You like it?" she asked as she handed me a mirror to inspect the work of art.

"I love it!" I responded. I reached in my purse to pay her. She waved me off.

"William already took care of it."

"A tip?"

"He took care of that too," she said as she handed me another card with a different address on it. I formed my mouth to ask a question, but she spoke before I could, "William told us not to answer any of your questions." I went with the flow.

I pulled up to 1100 Queen Street and walked into a beautiful nail salon.

"Ms. Bianca?" an older woman greeted me.

"Yes."

"I'm Noni, I'll be taking care of your nails today."

"Okay!" I said ready to accept this next stage of pampering. Noni filled the tub with water and motioned for me to sit and relax in the associated massage chair. She fixed me a mimosa as I relaxed. Then she hooked me up with the super deluxe fully involved mani-pedi. When she was done, she handed me another card with another address. I smiled at her and skipped off. This little day that William had planned was going perfectly.

72 King Street apartment D3. It was a residential property. I was a little skeptical, wondering if I had the correct address. I looked at the card a few times to make sure. I knocked on the door cautiously. A young lady who I recognized from church answered.

"Dee-Dee?"

"Hi Ms. Bianca!" she responded as she gave me a hug.

"You were expecting me?"

"Yes, I will be doing your make-up today," she stood with confidence as she spoke.

"Make-up?"

"Yes," she ushered me to a chair in her living room where she started strategically applying foundation, concealer, highlighter, lips, eyes, brows, and lashes—a full beat. She handed me the mirror when she was done, and I almost didn't recognize myself. She gave me a gorgeous natural glow, and I looked like I stepped off the page of a magazine.

"Oh my God! You are a true artist," I complimented her work.

"Well, God gave me a pretty nice canvas to work with." She winked at me. I hugged her and thanked her figuring it would be my last stop on this journey. She handed me another card with another address.

"Another one?" I asked.

She shrugged and smiled.

"If I asked you a question, would you answer?"

"Nope." She smiled, and she started to pack up her make-up. I giggled, shook my head, and went with it.

333 Church Street was an exclusive clothing store and as I walked in a man and a woman greeted me.

"Ms. Bianca?"

"Yep!"

"I am Gustaf, this is Bella," he said then handed me a prepaid credit card. "There is a 3000-dollar limit, get whatever you want."

"Excuse me?"

"Whatever you want," he said.

"Okay so do I need one outfit or two?"

"Whatever you want."

"Formal? Casual? Athletic?"

"Whatever you want."

"Shoes? Jewelry? Lingerie?"

"Whatever you want."

I looked at Bella hoping to get more information from her. She smiled. "Come, let me assist you." She escorted me around the store and anything I liked, she stashed it in a dressing room for me. I tried on a dozen outfits, shoes, jackets, and accessories. Then settled with five outfits, three pairs of shoes, two necklaces, one bracelet, three pairs of earrings, and two teddys that I planned to model for William later. When I was done, Bella handed me a beautiful dress with matching shoes, neither of which had I seen in the store.

"Put this one on now," she requested. I grabbed it and ran to the dressing room. The dress was perfect. It accented my figure well. I added my new bracelet and earrings to complete the ensemble then marveled at myself in the mirror. I was so excited I shrieked in joy.

Then I nonchalantly walked out of the dressing room and Bella handed me another card.

"Again?" I asked. "What could possibly be next?" She smiled at me. "I know, I know. You're not supposed to answer any questions." Gustaf grabbed my bags and escorted me to my car.

72 Union Street was a fancy restaurant on the Waterfront of Alexandria, Virginia. When I walked in three violinists started to play "Can't Help Falling in Love." William, James, and John were dressed in nice suits, and Chloe had a beautiful peach colored dressed which complimented mine. She stood with a big smile on her face and handed me the dozen roses she was holding in her hand. She formerly bowed her head, something she obviously picked up from an old movie.

"Why thank you Miss. Chloe," I playfully curtsied.

William walked over to me. "Bianca, I didn't think it was in God's will for me to meet my soulmate. Five years ago, I had given up on my dreams of having a family. Then Chloe walked into my life. Then you and the boys. My life has never felt more complete and I want to make our family official." He had tears in his eyes as he dropped down on one knee and pulled a little black box from his pocket. He opened it revealing a beautiful round two carat diamond ring with a halo.

"Oh my God," I gasped.

"Bianca, will you marry me?"

"Oh my God. Yes! Yes!" He stood up and kissed me, the kids jumped for joy, and the restaurant staff applauded. I tried to hold back tears not wanting to ruin my make-up, but I couldn't help it. It was the happiest moment of my life.

Chapter 8 – Cadence's Monsoon in 2017

I woke up on July 1st feeling like a new woman. As soon as I opened my eyes I jumped out of bed, ran to my purse, and opened my wallet. I marveled as I held in my hand my ticket to freedom and independence - my driver's license. I had just obtained it the day before. I still couldn't believe I passed on my first try. I had to look at it and make sure it wasn't a dream.

Someone lightly knocked on my door.

"Come in!" I yelled as I hurried to put my license back in my wallet.

My dad walked through the door. He held a tray with waffles, sausages, and orange juice. He placed the tray on my desk.

"I thought I heard you get up. Congratulations! This is your celebratory breakfast. And now that you have your license Cadence Ellison what are you going to do next?" my dad jokingly said in his best Ed McMahon voice while he held up an imaginary microphone.

"I'm going to Disney World!" I lovingly played along.

"And how do you expect to get there?"

"Um, a plane?"

"Or you could be driving in your new car!" He walked over to the window and drew back the curtains.

"What!? Seriously, dad stop playing," I followed him to the window and sitting in the driveway was a beautiful white Ford Mustang. "Oh my God! Oh my God!' I jumped up and down, "Thank you! Thank you!" I kissed and hugged him. Daniel walked in sleepy-eyed. I kissed and hugged him too.

"Well don't just stand there go check it out!" He handed me the keys. I ran out to the driveway and hugged the hood.

"Oh my God. I love it so much! Can I drive it?"

"It's yours!"

"Yes!" I jumped in the driver's seat, adjusted my mirrors, cranked on the engine, and though still in my pajamas, I high tailed it straight to Chloe's house.

"Beep! Beep!" I honked as soon as I pulled up. She opened up her window.

"What the hell?" she yelled down to me.

"Chloe look! I got a car! Get dressed! Let's go!"

"Oh my God!" She closed the window and, like superman, seconds later she was fully dressed and walking out the front door.

"Oh my God! I can't believe you got a new car. You are so lucky."

"Hop in girl. Let's go!" Chloe jumped in the passenger seat and we sped down the road. We went to the gas station first. My tank was half-full, but I was eager to pump my own gas for the first time. Chloe went into the store and got some junk food. Then we drove to the park. We sat there talking while eating Twizzlers and Skittles.

"Wanna drive?" I asked.

"I can't. I only have my learner's permit."

"Yeah, but I've got my license. You can drive while someone who has a license is in the car with you. Can you drive a stick?"

"No, but you can teach me!" Chloe grabbed my keys and we traded places. I explained how to raise off the clutch as she hit on the gas. She was able to pull out of the parking spot without problem. When she tried to switch into second gear, she had a little trouble and the car jerked forward. She tried again and there was improvement. I directed her to pull onto the main road which she did, and then we heard the sirens and saw the red and blue lights flash behind us.

"What did I do wrong?" Chloe asked as she put both hands up. I could see her anxiety rising.

"Nothing, I don't think. We weren't speeding."

A policeman ran over to the driver's side window and pulled his gun out aiming it at Chloe's head. "Don't move!" he yelled. I put my hands up too. I was shaking with fear. I could see tears swell up in Chloe's eyes.

His partner came to my side of the window, "Ma'am can you step out of the car please?" He opened the door for me, and I stepped out. He escorted me to the back of the car, "Ma'am are you in any danger?"

"No," I responded.

"Have you been kidnapped or hurt?"

"No. Why?"

"Why is that girl driving this car?"

"She's my friend. I was trying to teach…" I was interrupted by a large bang. I looked over and saw the first officer slamming Chloe on the hood of my car. Chloe's hands were laced on the back of her head and he held onto her wrist while he continued to point the gun at her.

"Don't move! Don't you fucking move or else I'll blow your brains out!" he shouted. Besides her shaking in fear she tried to remain as still as possible. The officer used his legs to spread her legs then he holstered his weapon and proceeded to pat her down.

"Hey, what are you doing?" I asked.

"She looks suspicious. We have a right to search suspicious looking people."

I knew his answer was bullshit. He didn't have a right to check her out without a proper warrant. And I looked way more suspicious than she did. I was the one in my pajamas. Chloe did nothing. She said nothing. She followed all their commands and yet here she was being slammed down, felt up, and threatened. I stood in shock realizing that all I had been told was a lie. Racism still very much existed, and Chloe was treated unfairly because of her skin tone. I wanted to do something, to say something, to help. I felt helpless as I watched Chloe's assault continue.

The officer handcuffed her then pushed her onto the concrete face down. He asked her question after question without giving her time to appropriately respond. The second officer tried to redirect my attention by blocking my view and asking me questions as well.

"Whose car is this?"

"Uh, it's, um, mine sir," I fumbled over my words too distraught to be legible.

"Do you have your license and registration?"

"Yes, it's here in my purse." I retrieved my purse and handed it to him.

"Why was she driving your car without a license?"

"She has her learners sir. I was teaching her how to drive a stick."

"Are you aware that in the state of Virginia in order to drive with a learner's permit you have to have someone over the age of 21 in the car? We have the authority to arrest her for driving without a license."

"No sir, I was not aware. But it wasn't her fault it was mine. I coaxed her into driving. If you want to arrest someone, arrest me."

"Hmmm," he said then he walked to his partner. They whispered to each other for about five minutes. I was allowed to walk freely while Chloe was still handcuffed on the ground.

When they were done the cop walked back over to me, "Okay ma'am we are going to let you off with a warning. Please don't let her drive your car again. Next time you both will be arrested."

They uncuffed Chloe without saying a word or helping her up. Then they left sounding the siren twice as they drove away.

I ran over to Chloe as soon as they left my vision, "Oh my God, Chloe. Are you alright?"

She sat on the curb still shaking. "Yes, I'm okay just a little spooked. You?"

I opened my mouth to speak, "I…I…" I couldn't form the words to express my mood and instead I started sobbing.

"Oh Cadence, it's okay," Chloe responded with sympathy. She wrapped her arms around me. She was the one who went through that crisis. I should have been comforting her, but instead she was comforting me.

"But it's not okay! How they treated you! I can't believe they did that! And for what? Cause your Black! That's just not fair!" I cried. The pain, anger, and shame I felt was overwhelming.

"Cadence, It's okay. I'm used to this kind of stuff."

"That's even more horrible. You shouldn't have to get used to it. It is 2017! This stuff should not be happening. How can people live with so much hate in their hearts? How can they treat people so bad because of their skin color and still look at themselves in the mirror? It just doesn't make sense."

"I don't know why. But I do know this, I am glad I have a friend like you that cares so much. You have the power to make a difference."

"What can I do? I just stood there like an idiot. I didn't even think to pull out my phone and record."

"Cadence, you are more powerful then what you realize."

Chloe's words woke a part of me that I didn't know existed. It awakened a drive to fight for justice and to right all the wrongs of society. I vowed to never again stand silent while someone else was being oppressed.

Over the next few months, I obsessed about my new awareness. I started a blog reflecting my views on racism in America. I donated money to the Innocence Project, the NAACP, and to HBCUs. I searched the internet looking for stories about racial injustice. I saw the pictures of Emmett Till. I watched documentaries about the 16th Street Baptist Church bombing where four little Black girls were killed. I watched movies like Roots, Now They See Us, Twelve Years a Slave, and Rosewood. I educated myself on the American history that had not been taught in school.

My brother and father thought I had lost my mind. Chloe made me promise not to tell them what happened in the park because she didn't want it getting back to her father. She knew if it got back to him, he would make a big deal out of it and it would be all over the news. She didn't want that kind of attention. I didn't agree, I felt our story needed to be heard and those cops needed to be punished; but I respected her wishes and kept silent. As a result, my family did not understand why I dramatically changed. I started wearing dashikis around the house and quoting Malcolm X. They'd roll their eyes and poke fun at me. But I ignored them. I was on a war path and I was fighting for what was right.

No one could watch television around me. I constantly pointed out the racist undertones behind each program.

A Christmas Story:
"See that's racist. How is it that the only Black person in the entire movie is the robber that Ralphie has to use a weapon against to defend his family?"

"Oh God. Cadence, the movie takes place in Indiana. There's not a lot of Black people in Indiana," Daniel attempted to defend his favorite Christmas movie during a Christmas in July marathon of the classic.

"Michael Jackson is from Indiana, and he was not a robber."

"He was a child molester."

"So, they say. But that could have been a ploy to bring another Black man down because he was too talented and becoming too wealthy."

Daniel rolled his eyes.

The Ten Commandments:
"Racist!" I yelled startling my father.

"Cadence, this is a religious movie. How is it racist?" my dad questioned.

"Everyone knows this Biblical story took place in Africa. Where are all the Black people in the movie?"

"Africa? It took place in…"

"Egypt, exactly. Egypt is an African country. You can see in ancient Egyptian art those people were brown colored with African facial features."

He ignored me.

Ninja Turtles:

"See that's Racist"

"How Cadence? How?" Daniel asked frustrated.

"The good guys, the ninja turtles are all named Raphael and Michelangelo, all after White artist. But the Bad guys, what are their names? Bebop and Rocksteady, named after Black art forms. Think about it."

"Cadence, it's a cartoon."

"Yes, they start bamboozling your mind at a young age."

Daniel brushed me off.

The news:

"See, that's racist. When the criminal is Black, they show their picture. When the criminal is White, no picture flashes on the screen. That is just the White man's attempt to keep the Black man down"

"Cadence," my dad chimed in, "I am a White man. I'm not trying to keep anyone down. I fought for this country to remain free in Operation Iraqi Freedom and Operation Enduring Freedom. Now over there in the Middle East, those are some oppressed people. Over here, no. You are fighting for people who don't want to achieve. If they wanted to be more than thugs and criminals, they would stop killing each other. You know how much Black on Black crime there is in this country? It's not the White man keeping Blacks down. It's the Black man keeping themselves down."

"Dad, there is White on White crime too. They just don't flash that on the news. Let's not forget, mom was killed by a White man. His picture wasn't on the news. The story didn't even make the newspaper. And what did they give him, a slap on the wrist. One year in jail and one year of probation."

"Your mom was killed by a drunk driver."

"Exactly! A White drunk driver. That's White on White crime. Had he been a Black man his picture would have been on billboards and he would have gotten 10 years in prison."

"Oh, Cadence." He shook his head unconvinced.

Then, I showed up to Chloe's house one night with an African headwrap and large wooden earrings in the shape of Africa. She cracked up laughing at the sight of me.

"What's up Afrika Bambaataa!" she mocked as she held up her fist. I had no idea who that was. But I remained straight-faced as I wrote down the name in my kente cloth encased notebook planning to google him later. She laughed more at my seriousness.

"What!?" I asked.

"Oh my God. Cadence, I love your enthusiasm; but…but…this is a whole new level of White empathy." Chloe laughed so hard tears poured out of her eyes. Her laugh was adorable and contagious. I couldn't help but to join in her amusement. I decided to hang up the African garb and go back to my own unique style of dressing. But the fire inside of me to fight for those who were treated unfairly still burned.

Chapter 9 – Chloe's Winter in 2018

The day we returned to school from winter break, I received an award from the principal for getting straight A's in the first semester of the school year. It was a nice start to the year 2018. I was proud of my 4.0 GPA. I worked hard to get it, harder than most. I wish things were equal where I went to school. I wouldn't have had to work so hard. But every year, there was always one teacher that was harder on me than my classmates. Freshman year, it was Mrs. Clements, my English teacher. It was supposed to be an easy class. According to the upper classmen, everyone got an A in her class and I loved English. While all the other kids clowned around, barely paid attention, and turned in assignments late, I was always interested, always participating, and always punctual. The upper classmen were right, she gave everyone an A. That is everyone except me. I remember looking at my final report card with a B in her class.

"Jeremy, what did you get in Mrs. Clements' class?"

"An A! We all did."

I knew Jeremy was not smarter than I. He asked me to help him with his final paper and it was awful.

"Cadence, what did you get?"

"An A. You?"

"I got a B."

"What? That can't be right. Your paper on *To Kill a Mockingbird* was genius."

"I know, right?" Cadence didn't realize it, but I knew why everyone got an A except me. It was because I was Black. Later that day, Daniel confirmed my suspicions. He told me that the same thing happened to a Hispanic girl in his class. She made a big fuss about it, and Mrs. Clements lowered her grade to a D. I wasn't going to make a fuss, but when my dad saw my report card, he did. He collected all of my work and took it to the principal proving my worthiness of an A. I was embarrassed by his gesture. I didn't want the negative attention. But in the end, I got my A.

Sophomore year, it was Mr. McFarley, my geometry teacher. Joshua was in my class that year. We both answered all the questions correctly on tests, but he'd get 100% and I'd get 99. I asked Mr. McFarley why he lowered my grade and his response was, because your lines were not straight. Compared to Joshua's work, they weren't crooked. I never told anyone about that little discrepancy. I just continued to strive harder making sure my lines and angles were perfect.

This year as a Junior, it was my gym teacher, Mr. Bates. He was blatant. "Chloe!" He'd yell. You're just as lazy as your ancestors. Come on pick up the pace!" he once yelled at me during a 1-mile race even though I came in third place. During archery, he threatened me, "Chloe, if I see you flash that bow near another person one more time, I'll send you straight to the principal's office and make sure you get suspended for attempted assault." My bow had been pointed only to the ground and target. I never flashed anyone. His comment shook me so much that I decided to just put the bow down. "That's a fail!" he yelled when I did so. I didn't argue. I just took it.

I was standing in his class trying to be discrete yet cooperative as to not give him a reason to yell. "Okay, today we are going to work on yawls leadership skills. We are breaking up in teams and one person will be selected to be the team's leader. You will guide your team on a series of exercises, and you will be graded based on your leadership skills. Team A, Anna you will lead. Team B, Sam. Team C, Brandon. And Team D…" he flashed an evil grin, "…Chloe." We engaged in several tasks -crossing our team across a spider web of intertwining ropes without using the same opening twice, creating an accurate drawing of Mr. Bates' office after only being allowed to look at it for three minutes, and directing a blindfolded teammate through a maze. Things started off a little rocky with our team but after a few minutes, we were running smoothly.

In the end, Mr. Bates gathered us and asked how we think we did and what team leader did the best. Several of my teammates and even people from other teams voted me as the best leader - complimenting me on how smoothly we completed each task and pointing out that I never raised my voice at any of my teammates. "Actually," Mr. Bates said, "Chloe did the worse out of all the leaders. Sam was able to take charge and establish dominance early in the exercises. Brandon fussed a lot, but his team completed their tasks quicker than any of the other teams. And Anna, she led the most cooperative team. Chloe was a poor leader. She did not establish dominance, she did not complete the tasks quickly, and she spent too much time listening to her teammates poor advice to be productive."

I didn't say anything. I refused to even look sad. I didn't want to give Mr. Bates the privilege of knowing that he got under my skin. Hunter, one of my teammates, leaned over to me and whispered, "I thought you did a great job."

I smiled knowing that he saw the discrepancy too. After class I changed clothes then exited the girl's locker room, "Hey!" I heard Hunter's voice call out from behind me.

"Hey," I responded.

"I know a great hang out spot out by the lake. Maybe you'd want to check it out with me sometime?"

"Like a date?"

"Yeah, a date."

I had never been asked out on a date before, so I was ecstatic, "Sure!"

"Cool. Pick you up on Saturday at seven?"

"Okay!" All the pain that Mr. Bates triggered disappeared at that moment. I couldn't wait to tell Cadence. But I had forgotten to give Hunter my number or my address. I knew he had football practice after school, so I decided to hang out by the boy's locker room and wait for him there. I wasn't trying to ease drop, but I heard their conversation as I waited.

"Heard you scored a date with Chloe? She's cute," one of his teammates spoke.

"Yeah!" another teammate agreed.

"Man, I'd love to fuck a Black girl. I bet they move like they dance, all freaky and shit. Wonder if they taste like chocolate," said someone else. They all laughed.

"She is cute, for a Black girl. But you know how it is with Black girls. You can fuck 'em but you can't take them home to mama," Hunter responded.

"True! True!"

I didn't need to hear anymore after that. I wasn't interested in being someone's experiment. The next few days I tried to avoid Hunter, but he kept on popping up unexpectedly.

"Hi Chloe!" his smiling face appeared when I closed my locker door.

"Hi," I mumbled then scurried away.

"Hi!" he appeared again when I stood up after taking a drink from the water fountain.

"Hello, umm. I'm late for class," then I ran off again.

"Hey girl! Are you avoiding me?" he appeared again when I walked out of the bathroom. I turned around slowly.

"No Hunter, I'm not avoiding you. I've just been busy."

"So, uh, about that date…"

"Look Hunter, I'm not going to be able to go out on that date with you."

"What? Why not?"

"Because you're an ignorant ass chauvinistic jerk" is what I really wanted to say. But instead I smiled and said, "Umm, I have an exam I have to study for."

"Well what about next weekend?" he asked.

"Ummm, my dad grounded me because…I bombed the last test. Uh yeah, I'm grounded for…the rest of the school year!" I was a really bad liar. Everyone in the school knew I was a straight A student. My name was posted on the honor roll every quarter. Nevertheless, he got the message and backed off.

**

"Valentine's Day is coming up! You got any plans?" Cadence suggestively spoke to me as we ate at the mall food court.

"No! You know I'm not dating anyone."

"You're not but you could be. What about Hunter? He seems to like you."

"He doesn't like me. He's only curious about tasting a little brown sugar."

"What you mean?"

"He doesn't like me as a person. He only wants to know what it's like to sleep with a Black girl."

"Mmmm…well, I think guys are scared to approach you. They are easily intimidated by brilliant girls. Maybe if you approached them, you'd find a good guy that likes you for you."

"Doubt it. What about you? You have yet to tell me about your date with Jeremy."

"Oh God," Cadence responded rolling her eyes.

"What? Jeremy's cute, and he's had a crush on you since freshman year. Bout time you gave that boy a chance."

"He's cute and all, but I don't really feel any passion, you know. He kissed me during the movie, and it felt awkward. Like I was kissing my brother. But we are not talking about me. We're supposed to be talking about you and your love life," she said as she playfully through a French fry at me.

"I have no love life." I threw the fry back. "Its Junior year all I want to do is focus on getting into NYU next year. Oh, that big city is calling my name. I plan to double major in Business and English. Then when I get out, I'm starting my own bookstore. One day, it's going to be as big as Barnes and Noble. Only better because it's going to be more high-tech. There will not only be Wi-Fi, but there will be large tablets built in the tables so you can order your coffee and little sandwiches from your table. Plus, there will be online chatrooms where you can talk about whatever book your reading with people who are reading the same book all over the world and when you talk, a 3D hologram of yourself will pops up on the table of the people you are talking to. The tablets will also work like an old-fashioned card catalog system where you can find the location of a desired book in the store. Plus…"

"Alright, alright. I got it. You're bookstore is going to be lit. But don't think you're slick. You tried to change the subject."

"Sure did! Did it work?"

"Yep, I'm really feeling your business ideas."

I smiled at the compliment. "So, what about you? What do you want to do?"

"I don't know," Cadence responded. "My grades aren't as good as yours. The only A I got was Freshman English. Maybe I'll go to community college. I like fashion design. Maybe something like that. Or maybe join the military like my dad. I'm not sure. But I do know I want a big family. I want to get married, have a bunch of kids, you know the American dream. Just not with Jeremy." Cadence made an exaggerated disgusted face. I laughed. Then a group of handsome guys walked by. They ignored me but smiled at Cadence.

"There you go," Cadence said to me.

"There I go what?"

"Those guys! They couldn't take their eyes off you."

I laughed, "Cadence, they were looking at you."

"I don't think so. They were looking at you. This is your opportunity. Go over there and get some digits."

I laughed, "Hell no!"

"Chloe!"

"What?"

"You're the one complaining, 'Oh I can't find a date.' Well now is the time to get one. Go!" I looked at her sideways. "Go!" she repeated.

"Okay fine." I stood up, straightened my clothes, and popped a stick of minty gum in my mouth. My heart beat a million miles per minute, but I forced myself to put one foot in front of the other to approach the group. *Chloe you are beautiful. You are smart. You are...what the hell are you thinking. You can't do this.* I turned back and Cadence mouthed to me, "go." I went.

As I approached, I sized up the group. *Okay, there are two White guys and one fair complexioned Black guy. Or maybe he's mixed. Who cares, he's cute. Look at his brown eyes and curly hair. Maybe I should try him.*

"Hi!" I said to the brown-eyed handsome stranger when I approached.

"Hey," he said back.

"Um, you seem pretty cool. Could I get your number and maybe call you sometime?"

He snickered then replied, "Sorry, I don't like darkies." Then he and all his friends laughed.

My pounding heart stopped and dropped. I felt the tears swell up in my eyes, but I held them back and instead walked away quickly.

Cadence stood up when she saw me retreat, "Chloe, what? What happened?"

I grabbed her, "Come on let's go." She followed me but repeatedly tried to get me to tell her what he said. I refused. But when we got to her car I cried, "He said he...he...doesn't like 'darkies.'"

"What an ass!" she responded. "You know what? His loss. His ignorance just caused him to lose the biggest blessing of his life."

Cadences words were nice, but they didn't make me feel better. I stared in the mirror that night feeling unattractive. I knew my chance at love was slim. Black American women have been portrayed as ignorant, ghetto, gold-digging, mouthy undesirables for centuries and as a result, I was more likely to get into Harvard Medical School then I was to get married to a good man. I tried to boost myself up. "It has nothing to do with you personally. That was just his preference. He's allowed to have a preference. There is someone out there who will prefer you." But I didn't believe it.

Chapter 10 – William's Frost in 2018

I didn't realize how much I missed James until he walked into Chloe's ICU room. His presence stirred up old memories of Bianca, the only person who I had ever fell in love with. Those memories hurt to reflect on; but I was glad James was there. Chloe and I both needed him.

James recommending the rape kit was hard on me. I knew I would lose my cool if I found out that Chloe was drugged and raped. I wasn't ready to face that possible reality. But he was right, and I knew the longer I waited on getting the testing done, the less evidence would be available. Chloe's third day in a coma was the first day I left her side. The doctors performed her vaginal exam and even though she was in a coma, I wanted her to have that privacy. I spent the next five days and nights by Chloe's side only leaving a few hours at a time to shit, shower, eat, and shave. She wasn't making much progress.

The stress of it all caused anxiety to build up. It felt like the walls in the room were closing in on me. I needed to get away. Home was not comforting. Not hearing Chloe wonder around and walking past Chloe's room at night knowing her bed was empty was too much for me to handle. I decided to go to the one place I could get my mind off my own problems and focus on someone else's - work.

When I stepped into the court room, my bailiff whispered to me, "Judge Wilcox, it's so good to see you; but are you sure you're ready to come back to work?"

"Of course, I am ready. I am fine."

Then Tracy and Ethan Conner walked into my courtroom. They were going through an ugly divorce. Ethan favored Bianca's ex-husband, Nathaniel, so much I took a double look at the last name to see if they were kin. As I listened to Tracy's pleas, I grew angrier at the sight of Ethan. She reported that he had been cheating, abusive, and purposely quit his job to avoid paying child support for their son. She looked distraught and hopeless. Ethan looked unmoved. He attempted to speak, but I didn't want to hear him. I made sure he was going to pay the price for leaving a woman to bear the burden of raising a child on her own. I was determined not to let another man get away with causing hurt and pain ever again. I sent him to jail for failing to pay the full amount ordered in child support.

My clerk pulled me aside after their case and asked, "Are you sure you are okay sir? I know you are going through a lot right now and…"

"I am fine!" I cut her off.

After that no other coworkers questioned my sanity, and I was able to finish the workday in peace. By the third case, I was back in my regular groove. My mind often wondered on James, John, Bianca, and most of all Chloe, but I was able to redirect my focus. At the end of the day, while I was in my chambers reviewing cases, built up anxiety flooded my heart, and I was no longer able to focus. I rushed back to the hospital.

"Anything change?" I asked the nurse who was catering to Chloe when I walked into the room.

"Oh, Mr. Wilcox the doctor was hoping that you would return so that he could talk to you in private."

My heart beat out of my chest. The palms of my hands started to sweat. I could feel my breath quicken. A doctor wanting to talk to me in private about the status of Chloe couldn't be a good thing. My vision blurred and I felt faint.

James walked into the room right on time. "Mr. William," he caught me. "Are you okay?"

"Yes, I just need to sit down."

"I'll get you some water and page the doctor. I know this is overwhelming," the nurse said as she pulled a chair over to me. I sat and James sat next to me in silence never letting go of my hand.

A few minutes later, Nurse Hamilton walked in with a physician who was holding a note pad.

"I'm Dr. Brown. I am the intensivist who has been taking care of Chloe. Are you Mr. Wilcox?" he asked James.

"Don't you think he's a little too young to be her father? I am Mr. Wilcox."

"Oh! Sorry sir. Well, Mr. Wilcox, it is nice to meet you. Is it okay we talk in front of…"? He looked at James.

"James. He's her brother," I introduced.

"Yes, of course. There is some private information I need to share. Is that okay."

"Yes. Anything you need to say to me you can say in front of him. He's family."

"Okay, well we have the results of Chloe's drug screen back. She had a mixture of alcohol, oxycodone, acetaminophen, tizanidine, and alprazolam better known as Xanax."

"Oh my God!" I said feeling faint again. I expected one maybe two drugs but five.

"Was the date rape drug in her system?" James asked.

"Well no but she had enough of the other things to cause amnesia, unconsciousness, and her current state, a coma."

"Well what about the rape test?" he asked.

"Um, yes, well that comes to my next two points. We did find semen in her vaginal vault."

"Whose was it?" James demanded.

"We are not able to determine that unless a sample of the potential donor is received. This case has been reported to the local authorities and they are working on it."

"Donor? You mean rapist," James asked. I was unmoved by Dr. Brown's overly rehearsed line that the police were looking into it. I knew police and Chloe's case was an afterthought locked up in a file cabinet.

"There were no signs of forced intercourse. Weather this was consensual or not is yet to be determined."

That pissed me off even more. I felt like he was trying to insinuate Chloe was promiscuous. I knew she had been withdrawn over the past several months, but she was not sleeping around. She had been too focused on her schoolwork to be sneaking around with boys. The fact that she was a straight-A student proved to me that she was a good kid and not a loose drug using teenager.

"You said there was a second point," I said through clinched teeth.

"Yes," he replied, "Umm, Chloe is pregnant."

"Excuse me?"

"Pregnant. Running a pregnancy test is standard during…"

"I got that but how? When? Is this the result of her…" I couldn't bring myself to say rape or sex. I didn't want to believe that Chloe experienced either. "How far along is she?"

"We are not sure how far along she is but with your consent we will do an ultrasound to find out."

I shook my head yes, and Dr. Brown left the room to order the testing.

"Can you believe that?" I asked James.

"Naw. Pregnant! I had no idea."

"It must be a mistake. Maybe I should ask them to run the test again."

"Let's see what the ultrasound says."

Dr. Brown came back with a machine. He lifted Chloe's gown and rubbed some blue gel on her belly. Her Belly was still flat. She couldn't have been that far along. I saw a head, an arm, and a foot. I heard the beating of the little baby's heart. I couldn't believe this little living creature existed in Choe's young abdomen. My emotions were everywhere. There was joy, pain, confusion, hurt, worry, love, and anger. I had so many questions. Who? When? Where? Why? Tears ran down my face. I had to get some air. Without saying a word, I left the room, hid in the bathroom, and gave myself a pep talk. "William, come on. You have to pull yourself together. Be strong. Chloe needs you. This baby needs you. And whoever did this to Chloe has to pay."

It took several minutes but I managed to collect enough energy to return to the ICU. By the time I got there, Dr. Brown was gone. James was crying and holding Chloe's hand.

"Dr. Brown said she's fourteen weeks and two days pregnant." He wiped his tears away with the back of his hand.

"So that's what? Like three months?"

"Yeah, a little over three."

"Do you have any idea who could have done this?"

"Imma put my money on Michael Harris. His dad was pretty aggressive when we went to confront him about the video."

"Video? What video?"

"Joshua's video."

"Can you get him to send it to me?"

"Bet," James pulled out his phone and began texting his requests. Minutes later he showed me the video of Michael and Chloe's argument.

"I think it's time we paid Michael another visit. This time we're bringing the police."

We drove to the police office and at the front desk slouched with his feet mounted on the desk was an officer I knew from court. His name was Joe, and he was an asshole. He often arrested or ticketed people, namely Black people, for the pettiest of offenses.

"Judge Wilcox," he said as he straightened. "What brings you down to this precinct?"

"My daughter, Chloe Wilcox, she has been raped. We think we know who did it, and we need your help."

"Well how do you figure she has been raped?"

"She was found unconscious and a rape kit at the hospital showed that she had semen in her," James chimed in.

'Well it could have been consensual."

"It wasn't!" I yelled. Other people may have seen my daughter as just some insignificant Black girl, but she was so much more than the color of her skin. She was smart, beautiful, kind, and good. She was motivated and she knew better then to let some boy ruin her entire future.

"We have a video that may be of some help," James spoke a lot more calmly than I felt.

"Okay, let me see this video."

James showed it to Joe as he pretended to look interested. "Well this doesn't show me anything. Plus, it is obviously edited. There is more to the video. Where did you even get this from?"

"It was sent to Joshua Bailey's phone from an unknown source."

"That doesn't help us out very much. You would need the original unedited video and the source. Consider hiring an IT guy. But this is not enough for any kind of prosecution. Do you have any more evidence?"

"You're the fucking cop. Aren't you the one who is supposed to be collecting evidence?" I yelled growing more and more frustrated with his narcissistic attitude.

Joe didn't respond. He just looked at me unmoved.

"Can you at least get a DNA sample from this guy to see if it's his semen?" James mentioned.

"We have to have a warrant for that."

"You want a warrant. I'll give you a warrant." I offered.

"You know that would violate code. You need an impartial judge to issue a warrant."

"But I'm the only judge in the area."

He shrugged. "Judge Wilcox, you and I both know this is not enough evidence for a warrant. Why don't you hire that IT guy and try to find the rest of the video and the source? Bring some more solid evidence, and we will talk to Judge Jenkins in Stafford county for the warrant."

I wanted to knock Joe off of his high horse and wring his neck, but James pulled me away and thanked Joe for his help.

'We obviously aren't going to get help here. Let's go to Michael's house. See if we can get more of the story from him."

I agreed.

Chapter 11 – Chloe's Summer in 2018

"Dad can I borrow the car to go to the mall?" I asked. I hated that I didn't have a car of my own. Cadence got hers a week after her 16th birthday and here I was seventeen and a half and I didn't have a thing. Money wasn't the issue. My dad made way more money than her dad. I got better grades then she did. And I was a way more responsible driver. But yet my dad, no matter how many valid points I presented would not budge. His excuse, "You're not ready to carry the responsibilities of having a car." That was some bullshit. I knew the real reason was because he wasn't ready for me to grow up. He still saw me as the little helpless girl he adopted eleven years ago. But that wasn't me anymore. I was growing, and I was ready to leave the nest and take on the world.

"Are you finished your chores?"

"Yes," I responded.

"Did you take out the trash?"

"Yes."

"Clean your room?"

"Yes."

"Do the dishes?"

"Yes! Come on Dad."

"Hmm, why do you need to go to the mall in the first place?" He tried his best to use any excuse to keep me locked up and sheltered from the world. I wanted to say feminine products. Any mention of that, he'd retreat and give me space. But I used that excuse the week prior. He'd know I was lying. So, I was honest, "I really need some new shorts. My ones from last summer are getting too small."

"Hmmm…okay. But no speeding. No joy riding. No drinking. No boys. No texting and driving. No loud music."

"Okay dad, I know. I know." I gave him a hug and kissed him on the cheek. Then I grabbed the keys and left. Being inside the house all day I was like a caged bird but driving down the highway felt liberating. I rolled down the windows just to feel the fresh air on my face.

The mall was crowded. It took a while to find a parking space and inside people scurried around like bees in a beehive. I decided to stroll through the chaos. I wanted to enjoy my little bit of freedom. I tried to drag out my shopping trip as long as possible. I was checking out some cute jean shorts in H&M when a nice baritone voice spoke from behind me.

"Hey Chloe."

I turned around and saw those beautiful dark eyes that I admired from a distance for the last 3 years. It was Michael Harris. I was stunned and speechless. I didn't even realize that he knew my name.

"Uh…uh…" My loss of words was embarrassing. I smiled and walked away to avoid further humiliation.

He followed behind me, "So, do you shop here often?"

I smiled.

"Do you speak?"

"Yes, I do."

"Your name is Chloe, right?"

"Yes, it is."

"Do you say more than three-word sentences?"

I giggled, "Yes."

"Okay, well maybe we could go out to lunch one day and talk some more?"

"Umm, like a date?"

"Yeah! Would that be cool?"

"Sure!"

"Okay, let me see your phone." I handed it to him. "Here's my number," he said as he typed. "Give me a call tomorrow, and we can make plans to meet up maybe Friday?"

"Yeah, that sounds good." I was beside myself. I couldn't believe that Michael Harris asked me out on a date. I took out my phone and immediately called Cadence. She would freak out when I told her, but the call went straight to voicemail. I couldn't believe it, the happiest day of my teenage life and Cadence forgot to charge her phone. I figured I'd talk to her later, but I was not able to reach her all night.

The next morning, I woke up tempted to call Michael at the break of dawn. I didn't want him to think I was thirsty, so I waited until 12:15.

"Hello." He sounded so sexy answering the call.

"Hey Michael. This is Chloe. How are you?"

"Chloe! I was hoping you'd call. I'm good. How 'bout you? What you up to?"

That was the start of a nice five-hour conversation. It would have been longer if my dad hadn't called me down for dinner. Dad and I always ate dinner together, he always insisted. There were no electronics allowed at the table because he wanted to talk to me and know all that was ongoing in my life, which was usually nothing.

"So, Chloe, you've been on the phone all day. Who were you talking to?"

"Cadence," I lied. He bought it.

"What is she fussing about?"

"Oh, you know. Same old same old."

He smiled, and I changed the topic onto him, his job, and his day. He was happy to vent about the stressors of work. He was the reason I wanted to major in business instead of law. His career had way too much drama, too much stress, and it seemed like only the scheming lawyers got rich. I didn't want that for my life. But I didn't mind my dad's stories. They were entertaining.

I could feel my phone vibrate in my pocket. I reached to answer it. "No electronics zone," William said as he noticed me reach. I finished diner and ran upstairs thinking it was Michael calling me back, but I saw Cadence's house number instead. She never called me on her house phone. Just as I made it to my room, she called again.

"Hello," I answered.

"Chloe," she whispered. "Sorry I didn't call you back last night. My dad took my phone away."

"Cadence, what did you do now?"

"He saw my final report card."

"How bad was it?"

"Well I passed but barely. I'm grounded for six weeks. He told me that I could study all the assignments and quizzes I missed to keep myself busy this summer. I just wanted to let you know so you wouldn't worry. I'll sneak a phone call here or there to check on you though." I heard Cadence's dad yelling for her in the background. "Shit! Gotta go. Love you, boo."

"Love you too." She hung up so fast that I wasn't able to tell her about Michael.

My first date with Michael was amazing. We met on Fridays for lunch. He looked handsome and smelled fresh. We talked, ate, and laughed. I didn't notice at school how funny and charming he was. I became even more infatuated with him. Plus, he kept calling me 'cutie'. Every time he said it, my heart jumped. Weeks went by, and we grew closer. For me, it was a dream come true.

I snuck over to his house one day while our parents were at work. We were supposed to be watching a movie on Netflix but instead we were making out. His hands reached for the button on my jeans. I grabbed his hand and moved it away.

"What's up? We've been dating for weeks now. Aren't you ready?"

I didn't respond. I just sat up, crossed my legs, and folded my arms. I wanted to have sex with him, but I wanted to be in a committed relationship with him first.

"Don't be like that," he said as he stroked my cheek. "I really like you, and I thought you liked me."

"I do like you."

"So, what's up?"

"Nothing's up. I just don't want…"

"Don't want what? Me?"

I rolled my eyes. "You're not even my boyfriend."

"Oh, here we go with the boyfriend stuff again. What does it matter? I like you. You like me. That's all we need."

I stiffened again.

"Fine, you want me to be your boyfriend. That's it. We are boyfriend and girlfriend now."

He leaned over and tried to kiss me, and I turned away. I did not want to be asked to be someone's girl so rudely. He sighed and buried his head in the pillow. "Girl I can't believe you gonna do me like that." He moved to the other side of the couch and folded his arms in anger. I felt bad. I didn't want him to be mad at me. I crawled over and kissed him on his neck.

"Naw girl. I'm not feeling this. You can't keep on teasing me like that. You gonna have to stay over there, and we are just gonna have to be friends." I didn't want to be friends. I wanted to be his girl. The tears began to form in my eyes. I didn't want him to see me cry so I left. I was hoping he'd rush after me and apologize like the leading man in a romance movie, but he didn't. He didn't move an inch. Still sitting with folded arms. I tried to call the next day, no answer. A day later, also no answer. I got the message and stopped calling.

A week later, he called me like nothing happened.

"Hey cutie, what you doing?"

"I'm looking at colleges for next year."

"How about Old Dominion? That's where I'm going."

"You want me to go with you?"

"Yeah, you my girl, right?" That was all he had to say, and I was infatuated again. Two nights later I had sex, for the first time willingly, with him in the back of his car on an old dead-end country road. And for the next few weeks we were having daily rendezvous.

Cadence promised that she would call me back, but she wasn't able to do so until she was officially off punishment. I was happy to hear her voice. I wanted to tell her everything.

"Hey love," I answered.

"Hey boo, I am finally off of punishment. Hallelujah! That was the longest six weeks of my life. Anyway, I am so happy. I got off punishment right in time for the anniversary of Heather Heyer's death."

"Heather who?"

"Heather Heyer, you remember last year the girl who died in the Charlottesville right? Anyway, this year they are organizing a peaceful protest commemorating her and opposing racism. You want to go?"

"Sure!"

"Cool, I'll pick you up tomorrow morning, like 8?"

"Okay!"

"Okay, love you, bye."

"Love you too."

I still didn't get a chance to tell her. But I figured the next day on the long drive to Charlottesville I'd be able to fill her in on the last six weeks. I was wrong. The entire way she was filling me on the drama with her family. Daniel tore his ACL during a basketball summer camp for college and he'd be out for possibly the entire season. He was miserable moping around the house and being an asshole. His girlfriend of three years dumped him as a result. That made him more agitated. She and her dad had been diligently going to church trying to pray the misery away; but it didn't seem to be working. Daniel was more interested in treating himself with alcohol and marijuana. He had been hanging out with the wrong crowd, getting in trouble with the police, and ruining his life.

I was completely involved in the story. I couldn't believe Daniel, who was a brother to me as much as he was to Cadence was getting into so much trouble. Before I knew it, we were pulling up to the protest.

"No justice! No peace! No racist police!" We could hear the chants blocks away. The unity in the voices made my heart race. For the first time in my life I was proud to be a Black American. It felt good to see signs with the words "Black is Beautiful," "I Am A Man," and "Diversity Is What Makes America Great!" Cadence parked in a lot a few blocks away from the action. Before she got out the car, she pulled her hair up into a ponytail, and put on her earrings, the wooden African shaped ones.

"What? You kept the African earrings?"

"Girl yes. These things are hot. Besides, we all come from the motherland anyway. It's just that my ancestors from there are more distant than yours." She winked at me.

I giggled and shook my head. "Well they do look cute on you."

"I know. Here is your sign and here is mine."

My sign read "My Life Matters," and hers "I May Never Understand, But I Stand!" We marched and chanted side by side. We walked with a diverse people. There were Black, White, Hispanic, and Asian people. We all ignored the opposing White Supremacist protestors who yelled obscenities while they carried Swastikas and Confederate flags. We ignored the police officers who were aggressively positioned in riot gear just waiting to attack. It was terrifying and beautiful.

A few hours after our arrival, a tall Black man ran through the crowds shouting, "Ay, someone out here slashing tires!"

"Oh shit! You think they might get my car?"

"I don't know but let's go check."

We made our way through the crowd and to the parking lot. We saw a few masked people jump into a white van and speed off. There were several tires in the parking lot that had been slashed. God must have been looking out for us because it looked like the perpetrator vandalized the cars in the order in which they were parked. On our row, they stopped only two cars before us. We decided that maybe it was time to leave before we became the next target.

"Oh my God! That was amazing!" I yelled as we got into the car. "To see so many people fighting against injustice. It made me feel so alive. Did you see that 'Black is Beautiful' sign? Did you see how respectful people were to me? People were calling me 'My Beautiful Black Sista' and 'Nubian Queen.' It made me feel so…so…. beautiful! I've never felt that way before."

"You've never felt beautiful before?"

"No. I never felt I was. People say I'm kind of cute. But they never tell me I'm beautiful. It almost feels like they see my chocolate skin as a curse. Like I'd be beautiful if I was a lighter complexion. Like my dark skin is ugly. I'm only viewed as cute for a Black girl but never seen as a beautiful woman. For the first time, today, I actually felt like a beautiful woman."

As I was talking Cadence pulled onto a side street and put the car in park. She turned off the car and looked at me. Her breathing quickened and she looked anxious, upset, and excited all in one.

"Chloe, I've always thought you were beautiful." She stroked my cheek and continued, "You are the most beautiful woman I know."

Then she leaned over and kissed me on the lips. It was a gentle peck. I could feel her heart pounding rapidly. She kissed me again but with more intensity and passion. I pulled away in surprise. Cadence gasped in fear.

"Cadence, what was that?" I questioned.

Tears formed in Cadence's eyes. For the first time of me knowing her, she had trouble finding words to speak. "Oh…I am so…uh…sorry. I didn't…I did not, uh, mean to…"

"No, don't be sorry. It's okay. I mean I love you. But not like that…How long have you known?"

"Known what?" Cadence responded while trying to hold back her tears.

"Known that you were gay? Or bi? Or tri?"

She let out a small giggle. "Tri?"

"Yeah, I mean do you only like girls, or boys and girls, or are you not sure what you like?"

"I'm quite sure I'm all lesbian. I think I've always known. I don't have any attraction to boys, only girls. It's been like that since

I could remember. I tried to ignore it. Tried to hide it. Tried to pray it away. But it's me. It's who I really am."

"Well, you don't have to hide it anymore."

"Ha! Speak for yourself. When my dad finds out, he's going to flip."

"You never know. He may be supportive."

"I'm not ready for this to come out yet. Can you not tell anyone just yet?"

"Your secret is safe with me. Chloe and Cadence for life?" I held up my pinky.

"Chloe and Cadence for life!" She entangled her pinky with mine.

Between Cadence inching her way out of the closet and Daniel's fall, it would have been inappropriate to tell her about my blooming relationship with Michael. I kept it to myself and decided to be her support. The rest of the summer it was me and Cadence or me and Michael, but never was it me, Cadence, and Michael.

Chapter 12- Chloe's Autumn in 2018

I laid in Michael's arms one day after we had just finished making love. I was high off that post-sex endorphin rush. I was falling in love with him. I wanted to tell him but knowing that he'd be going away to college in a week was anxiety-provoking. He stroked my arm while staring up at the ceiling fan. I wanted to know all of him. I wanted to know his thoughts, desires, and dreams.

"What are you thinking?" I asked.

"I'm thinking about me going to college next week."

As he said it my anxiety started to rise. "Yeah, what about it?"

"Well, it's going to be hard to maintain this when I am away. Maybe we should break up now and just be friends. You know. I don't want to hold you back."

I sat up trying to compute the words he said, "Excuse me?"

"I really like you Chloe, but I want to break up."

Yep, I heard him correctly. I rose and started to get dressed as tears filled my eyes.

"Chloe." I ignored him. "Chloe!"

"What!?"

He stood up and held me as the tears poured down my face. His touch was comforting. But I knew what was really up. He was ready to move on and have fun with some college girls. There was no room in his heart for me, only room in his pants. I broke away from him and left. I planned not to call him ever again. I was heartbroken. I wanted to tell Cadence, but I hadn't even told her about the affair; how would she understand the break-up.

Plus, Daniel was just placed on two years of probation and court mandated rehab. He was lucky my dad was the judge on his case. He could have been sentenced to years in jail for his actions. He was arrested for robbing a house to get money for drugs with some of his friends. He was high on cocaine at the time.

**

Michael left for college without even a phone call to say bye. And for me, senior year of high school started. Joshie and I were sitting at the lunch table. Cadence walked in late and looking panicked.

"You okay?" I asked her.

"You got a pad? I came on early this month."

"Oh God," Joshie said as he scooted further from us. "I love you guys, but I don't need to hear about your girlie problems."

I laughed and shook my head, "Yeah, here I keep one in my purse at all times."

"Thanks love," she said as she did a quick closed leg shuffle to the bathroom.

I laughed and shook my head as she walked away. Then I thought, *when was my last period?* I calculated in my head and realized it had been six weeks. Fear filled my heart. *Could I be pregnant?* I shook off the thought. Maybe I was late because I was stressed. Michael and I had been safe. We usually used condoms and the few times we didn't he pulled out. I couldn't have been pregnant, but I thought it would be in my best interest to get tested just in case.

Cadence usually drove me to and from school. On the way home I asked if I could stop by the store. It took creativity to lose her in the store and purchase the pregnancy test without her seeing. I got home before my dad did and I peed on the stick. It was the longest two minutes of my life. I paced back and forth checking each second to see if there were two lines or one.

I saw a second line forming. "No, it can't be." I read the directions four more times to make sure that I was understanding. Two lines meant pregnant. One line, no pregnancy. I decided to wait five more minutes to see if the second line would disappear. It didn't.

I googled pregnancy tests and found that it is more accurate in the mornings. I decided to take the second test the next morning just to confirm. I couldn't sleep that night. I tossed and turned wondering about the little baby that may have been growing inside of me. I worried about how Michael would react. I needed to talk to someone but had no idea who. Cadence was going through too much in her own life she wouldn't be able to handle my mess too. Michael was away. Joshua wouldn't know what to do. I couldn't go to William because he'd kill me. I couldn't go to James because he'd kill Michael. I never felt so lonely.

I jumped out of bed an hour before my alarm went off and peed on the second stick. Yep, two lines. That confirmed it. I was pregnant. My feelings were mixed. On one hand, I was carrying a new life with a man that I loved. On the other hand, I was young, unwed, and I had no idea how to be a mother. Bianca was the closest thing I had to a mother while growing up, but she was no longer there. I knew I needed a mother to help me with this unforeseen circumstance. I decided that I was going to find my birth mother and enlist her for help.

Cadence picked me up right on time for school that day; she was always on time.

"Hey girl, what's new?" she asked as I hoped in the car. I formed my mouth about to reveal everything. But I stopped thinking that maybe I should tell Michael first.

"Girl, I just talked to you last night. Nothing's new. And you?"

"I talked to Daniel last night. He sounded good. He's making friends and staying clean. He's been learning a lot about himself and addressing some issues that were deep routed in his heart. The loss of mom really took a toll on him, but he'd been holding it in for years. He thought he needed to be strong for me and dad. His only outlet was basketball. And when he lost that. He felt like he lost everything. I never knew he felt that way."

"Me either. Well I am glad he's doing better. I'll keep him in my prayers."

As we walked into school, Jamie, the captain of the girls' basketball team walked past.

"Hey Cadence." She waved in a very flirtatious manner.

"Hi…uh…Jamie," Cadence responded obviously flustered.

I nudged Cadence. "She's cute, huh."

"Yeah," Cadence had stars in her eyes.

"Well go talk to her."

Cadence looked at me like I was tripping.

"What? She obviously likes you."

Cadence shook her head, snickered, and walked ahead of me.

"What?" I taunted.

"I've gotta get to class. Love you."

"Love you too."

When I was with Cadence I didn't think about my problems. I was too busy laughing and joking around with her. But being alone in my first period class, all I could think about was the pregnancy, Michael, my dad, and my birth mother. I couldn't even remember my birth mother's name.

I texted Michael, "We need to talk."

The school day went by, but he didn't return the text.

When I got home, I called him. No answer. Over the next few days, I kept calling and texting with no response. I figured he blocked me. That weekend, I spent the night over Cadence's house, snuck in her brother's room and took his phone. He wasn't allowed to have his cell phone at the rehab facility so I knew it would be somewhere in his room. I texted Michael from Daniel's phone, "Michael, this is Daniel. There is something wrong with Chloe. She needs you promptly. Emergency 911!"

Minutes later, Michael was calling my phone. I went to the bathroom to answer.

"What's wrong?" he asked nonchalantly.

"I'm pregnant."

"Huh?"

"I'm pregnant. I've been trying to call you, but you wouldn't answer. What's up? You blocked me or something?"

"Naw, just been busy. You're pregnant? What are you trying to say? Is it mine?"

"Of course, it's yours. You're the only person I've been with."

"Mmmm, so what? You want me to pay for the abortion or something?"

"Excuse me?"

"An abortion. You're not keeping it right?" His indifference was pissing me off.

"I haven't decided on getting an abortion."

"Well I'm not ready to be a daddy so you gotta do something. I'll send you the money. I'll go with you to get it done. Whatever you need. But I'm not having a baby with you." Then he hung up on me.

I hyperventilated. I was even more lost about what to do. Cadence knocked on the door.

"Chloe, you okay?"

I pulled myself together enough to respond, "Yeah, I'll be out in a minute." My voice cracked, and I knew Cadence didn't buy my attempt to ensure her things were okay. She stood by the door and empathetically listened. I splashed water on my face, took some deep breaths, and opened the door with a plastered smile on my face. She suspiciously looked at me, aware that something was wrong. But she didn't say anything. She wrapped her arms around me and held me close. I started to cry. She held me tighter.

"Chloe, I don't know what's going on with you but I'm here when you're ready to talk. I love you. Whatever you need. I'm here." It was exactly what I needed to hear.

"I…I…" I wanted to tell her everything, but my emotions were too unstable. The only thing that came out was, "I need to find my birth mother."

"Okay…okay…what do you know about her?"

"Not much."

"I bet Joshie can help." I smiled and nodded.

On Sunday, I snuck through my dad's files and found my social security card, birth certificate, and adoption papers. My mother's name was Maybeline Price, and I was born Chloe Price at Mercy Hospital in Baltimore, Maryland. I snapped pictures of the documents with my phone and sent it to Joshie. He was happy to help. Within a week he was able to find my mother's last known address, and I convinced Cadence to skip school and drive me to Baltimore to see her. I planned to tell both my mother and Cadence everything together. I figured between the two of them, I'd get the support that I needed and be able to do what I really wanted to do, keep the baby.

Michael's father obviously didn't care that William was Chloe's father or a judge. He slammed the door in his face too. But as we turned to leave, I saw Michael staring at us through his bedroom window. He motioned for us to meet him down the street.

We got into our car and drove to the corner so that Michael's father would think we left. Ten minutes later, Michael was knocking on the window. William got out first with folded arms and an intimidating scowl. I got out and stood to Michael's side matching William's countenance and posture.

"Mr. Wilcox sir, I never meant for Chloe to get hurt. We…we…was just having fun. We…no I should have been more careful."

"Fun?" I was fuming. Chloe was never meant to be his plaything.

"Yeah, this summer? We hooked up a few times. Then she got pregnant. She said I'm the father but…"

"But what? What are you trying to say? If Chloe says you're the father, then you're the father and you will be taking full responsibility for the baby," William cut in.

"We didn't come here to talk about the summer," I added. "We care about what happened at the party. We know Chloe was drugged and raped and we have evidence that you did it."

"The party? Nothing happened at the party," Michael objected.

"This video tells us different!" I held my phone so Michael could see as I replayed the argument.

"Yeah, we were arguing about the baby. She wanted to keep it, but I wanted her to abort. Nothing happened though. We went to the room. Talked for a few minutes then I left."

"The rape kit tells us different."

"Rape? There was no rape. We didn't even have sex that night."

"Really? Are you willing to provide a DNA sample to prove your innocence?"

"Sure, what do I have to do?"

"Come to the police station with me and volunteer your sample."

Michael agreed and we all rode to the station. He willingly gave his sample. We dropped him off at the corner where we initially met then William and I went back to the hospital.

Chloe's nurse informed us that Chloe already had a visitor and that only one of us could go in. William suggested I go. He was overwhelmed and wanted to go home and take a shower. When I got to the room, Cadence was holding Chloe's hands and singing "His Eye is on the Sparrow." She had a beautiful voice for a White girl. She smiled as I walked in. I stood silent as she finished her song.

"I can't dance to save my life," Cadence started. "And Chloe can't sing. But when we are together, our talent is untouched. I sing, she dances, and the world is inspired. She loves when I sing that song. She said it makes her feel safe."

"My mom used to sing that song to her," I held back tears. Cadence nodded her head in understanding.

"Did you know?" I asked. "Did you know that Chloe was pregnant?"

Cadence looked at me as tears filled her eyes, "I didn't know. But I suspected. A few times on our way to school, I'd have to pull over so she could vomit. She never told me she was or who she was pregnant by. I figured she'd tell me when she was ready. I just stood by her side and waited. Maybe if I had confronted her and helped her sooner, she wouldn't...wouldn't be..."

"Chloe is lucky to have you as a friend. You did nothing wrong."

Cadence nodded.

We sat and both sang to Chloe. We heard the beeping from her heart monitor quicken as we sang. A nurse came in and checked the equipment.

"Looks like Chloe is breathing over the ventilator."

"Is that bad?" I asked.

"No, it's good. It means she's starting to breath on her own. Whatever you are doing, it is working." It was the first sign of progress Chloe made since she was admitted. Cadence and I smiled at each other then we hugged.

"I gotta call Mr. William and give him the good news."

I did, and he immediately came to the hospital. Cadence volunteered to take me to William's house so I could shit, shower, and shave. It had been two days since I bathed. After my shower, I walked into Chloe's bedroom wearing just a towel. My bags were in

Chloe's room. Cadence was sitting on Chloe's bed looking at a picture on the nightstand. It was a picture of them at some protest. She turned her head and flashed an innocent welcoming smiled when she saw me. She glanced over my body and gasped. Unshyly she walked over and touched the disfiguring scars on my abdomen.

"Oh my God, what happened?"

It was a typical reaction that I got from people when I was shirtless. Initially it bothered me but overtime I got used to it. Sometimes with the ladies, it got me play. They'd ask, I'd tell, they'd feel sorry for me, and give me some pussy. Hay, you play with the cards you were dealt. That was my hand.

"Chloe didn't tell you?" I asked.

"No!"

"But she told you about me?"

"Yeah."

"And she told you about my mother?"

"Yeah, little stuff, not details."

"Well…" My phone rang interrupting my story. It was William. I answered, "More good news?"

"No, something is wrong. Chloe is bleeding."

"We're on our way."

When we got to the hospital, we found William pacing back and forth in the ICU waiting room.

"What happened?" I asked.

"I was just sitting there talking to Chloe and I noticed a lot of blood on her sheets. I called for the nurse who started to examine her. The blood was coming from her private area. The doctor was called in. He's examining her now."

"Let's pray," Cadence suggested. We held hands and Cadence spoke, "Heavenly father, you are an all-knower, a miracle-worker, a way-maker. We come together in prayer asking for you to help Chloe Wilcox. Touch her body and heal her, in the name of Jesus. Heal her mind, body, heart, and her womb. And please Lord provide us strength and comfort during this trial. In Jesus name we pray. Amen."

"Amen."

A few minutes later the doctor came out. "Are you the family of Chloe Wilcox?"

We all stood. "Yes."

"I am sorry to inform you, but she lost the baby." I immediately started crying. "Her body is under a lot of stress. It just wasn't strong enough to maintain the pregnancy."

"I thought she was doing better?" Cadence asked.

"She is making slow progress. We still have a long road ahead."

After the miscarriage, we stayed by Chloe's side in shifts. I had the day shift, Cadence stayed with her after school for the evening shift, and William had the night shift. On my shift, a social worker came to Chloe's room and informed me that Michael was not a match to the semen that was found inside of Chloe. It was painful to hear and until Cadence showed up for her shift, all I could think about was how we could find who's semen it was.

I told Cadence the results, and we brainstormed about how we could find the culprit.

"All we have is this video," I said. Cadence and I looked at it a dozen times to see if there were any more clues. There weren't.

"Okay, who sent the video?" I asked.

"Unknown number."

"Well isn't Joshua a computer geek? Can't he trace it?"

"He's more of a math nerd then a computer geek, but he can do some stuff. He said that he tried but couldn't find the source."

"Damn, well maybe we should hire someone who can trace it."

"Yeah, but why would the villain send the evidence?"

"Maybe he was trying to set up Michael. Maybe it's one of Michael's enemies who did this."

"Maybe," Cadence thought. "Well, it was Jeremy Carter's party. He provided the drugs used at the party. And he was the one who called me and told me Chloe was at the hospital. Maybe we should try to get some evidence from him."

"Cool, where is he?"

"In jail."

"What? For what?"

"Possession of drugs with intent to sell. When he called the ambulance for Chloe, not only did the EMTs show up but the cops too. They found all kinds of stuff, ecstasy, cocaine, marijuana, and prescription drugs. Plus, he was hosting a party with underage drinking. His family didn't have enough money for bail, so he's stuck until his hearing in a couple of weeks."

"Bet! How bout I go to the police station and request a DNA sample from him while he is still in jail? How 'bout you find someone who can trace the video?"

I went straight to the police station. I was happy to see that Joe was not at the front desk. In his place was a jolly looking man in uniform. He greeted me with a smile, "Hi! How can I help you?"

"My sister's friend, Jeremy is in your custody, I was wondering if I could visit with him."

"Hmmm, let me see," he started typing on his computer, "What's Jeremy's last name?"

"Umm, Carter, Sir."

"Hmmm, Jeremy Carter," he continued to type, "Ah hah, he's being held at Regional County Jail. Here's the address," he wrote on a paper, "And his inmate number. Oh, and here's the website. You'll need to go on the website to schedule a visit. Anything else I can do for you sir?"

"Umm, yes. How can I leave an anonymous tip about a crime?"

"You have a tip?"

"I know someone who does." The cop was nice, but I didn't want him to get suspicious about my interest in Jeremy.

"Oh, well just have your friend call this number," he wrote the number on the same sheet of paper. "It's our tip line."

"Thank you, sir." I took the paper and thought, *finally a police officer who actually is doing his job, to serve and protect.* From my car, I called the tip line and let them know that I had suspicions that Jeremy Carter was involved in the rape of Chloe Wilcox. And when I got to William's house, I made an appointment to pay Jeremy a visit the next day. Cadence agreed to go with me.

I picked her up and we drove to Regional. We had to leave all our things in a locker. Keys, cell phones, purses, and wallets were not allowed in the visiting room. In the room, we were directed to sit in front of a monitor. Jeremy's face appeared in the monitor.

"Hi Jeremy," Cadence spoke into the phone.

"Cadence," Jeremy nodded. "Who's your friend?"

"This is James, Chloe's brother."

"Oh, what's up?" Jeremy nodded at me. He didn't look intimidated or threatened by my presence. His body language at our introduction showed no signs of guilt.

"What happened to Chloe at your party?" I asked.

"I'm not sure. All I know is we were all partying and having a good time. I walked into my bedroom to get some more weed from my stash and Chloe was laying on my bed naked. I walked over to her and shook her, but there was no response. I leaned over to see if she was breathing. She was but barely. I yelled for everyone to get out of my house. I didn't want anyone to take the heat for her overdose. Everyone left except for Anna…"

"Who's Anna?"

"My girlfriend. I told her to leave too but she wasn't having it. She threw some clothes on Chloe while I called 911. The ambulance came and took Chloe to the hospital. That's when I called you," he looked at Cadence.

"And then?"

"Then nothing. I mean the cops came, tried to arrest me, and Anna but I admitted that all the drugs in the house were mine, and Anna had nothing to do with it. And here I am."

"Who sent the video?"

"What video?"

"The video that got sent to Joshua's phone."

"I don't know anything about a video." It looked like he was telling the truth but like my mom always said, "trust but verify."

I called William and told him of all our progress. He called the station to follow up. My tip was taken seriously, and Jeremy had been tested while in custody. The results were pending.

Chapter 14 –James' Spring in 2011

I was teased a lot in middle school. I was tall, skinny, uncoordinated, and I loved Jesus. My bookbag was way too big for my frame. On my back, I looked like I'd tip over at any moment. Not only did I carry a full load of schoolbooks, I always had my Bible in my bag too. I didn't have many friends to hang out with, so I usually had my face between the pages of God's word. My classmates nicknamed me Jesus' giraffe.

I loved to sing. At thirteen I had the unique luxury to sing in both the children's and adult choir. I was singing every Sunday. It was the first service of first Sunday and I was leading the choir in one of my favorite gospel songs, "Long as I got King Jesus." I could feel the Holy Spirit burning inside me. As I continued to sing, my overwhelming joy affected others. People in the sanctuary started shouting, crying, and praising in response to the song. And the fire inside me burned more until I started stomping, crying, and shouting too. The love in that church erased the pain I endured from being bullied throughout the week. "It doesn't matter what my peers say about me, I know I am wonderfully made and loved by God," I halfway sang, halfway shouted, and 100 percent believed.

"Yes Lord! Thank you, Lord!" Pastor Charles clapped and praised as he made his way on stage. That was the choirs signal to march our way off stage so he could begin the sermon. I was still spirit filled when I danced off the stage. As I calmed, I saw my mother sitting next to William. They both glanced at me with a twinkle of pride in their eyes. It was good seeing them together. It felt like family. Chloe had a big smile on her face as she enthusiastically waved at me. I waved back. John was lost in his own world playing games on his tablet.

Pastor spoke, "Yes Lord! Long as I got you, I don't need nobody else. Aren't you glad that Jesus is your friend? He can be your lawyer, your doctor, your mother. Anything you need you can find it in Jesus. Amen?"

"Amen," the church responded.

"Now, before we get started with today's sermon, I want to congratulate William and Bianca on their recent engagement. It has been beautiful watching the love grow between these two souls. And let's pray that they are blessed with a long, happy, and successful marriage."

Church members cheered, and a few people who were near gave William handshakes and Bianca hugs congratulating them on their milestone. Church was nice. Pastor talked about the resilience of God's people. He preached from Matthew 7:24-27, "Everyone then who hears these words of mine and does them will be like a wise man who built his house on the rock. And the rain fell, and the floods came, and the winds blew and beat on that house, but it did not fall, because it had been founded on the rock. And everyone who hears these words of mine and does not do them will be like a foolish man who built his house on the sand. And the rain fell, and the floods came, and the winds blew and beat against that house, and it fell, and great was the fall of it."

His message was that people who have faith, a relationship with God, and follow the teachings of the Bible when trials and tribulations come their way, they are able to stand strong and survive. But those who are not following God, when trials and tribulations come their way, it destroys them. I thought about my bullies at school. They were my storm and yet I had not fallen. I figured I must have been doing something right and I was looking forward to the day when God would make my enemies my footstool.

After church, William took us all out to brunch then dropped us off at home. I immediately ran to my room, jumped out of my church clothes, and turned on my video game. John followed me into my room.

"Can I play?"

"I just got on!"

"So?"

I sighed. I had been waiting to play *Batman: Arkham Asylum* all day and it was a one-man game, so he was short. "Go play on your tablet. I'll be done in an hour."

He rolled his eyes and left. I put my headphones on to block out anymore interruptions from him or my mom. I didn't notice the knock at the door. But after my mom opened it, I noticed that she was fussing at someone. I figured it was a Jehovah's witness, she didn't mind challenging those unwanted guests in a game of who interprets the Bible better.

There was a knock on my door. "Come in!" I said as I took my headset half off to hear what whoever was disturbing me had to say. It was John again. "It hasn't even been twenty minutes!" I fussed before he could speak.

"Dad is here. He wants to see you."

I rolled my eyes. I hated that man. I knew John was too young to remember, but Nathaniel was an angry man. He'd beat on Mom for the dumbest of offenses. His food was too cold, she took too long at the grocery store, her hair wasn't done to his liking, she asked for money to get her hair done. Mom couldn't win for trying. There were a few times when I stepped in attempting to guard mom. He beat me too. I was glad when we left.

"Tell him I don't want to see him."

"He wants to give you a birthday gift."

That deadbeat didn't even realize my birthday was still two months away. "Tell him I don't want anything from him."

"Okay," John shrugged and walked out the room defeated.

"Pop pop," I heard the sound of the gun and figuring it was one of the criminals in my video game, I ignored it.

"Pop pop," I heard louder followed by a gut-wrenching screech that I knew was not part of the video game. I snatched off my headphones and ran into the living room in just enough time to see Nathaniel shoot a third bullet into my mom's head who had been laying on the ground pleading for her life. John was laying on the couch with his eyes opened and blood pouring from his chest.

I turned to run. "Pop pop," I heard again. There was a burning pain in my stomach. I saw the blood as it splattered in front of me. Then I fell. My vision was fading to black, but I could hear Nathaniel's footsteps as he ran towards me. He kicked me to see if I would move, but I was too weak to wince. I heard him run out the door. Then I completely lost consciousness.

**

"If you can hear me squeeze my hand!" a nurse yelled at me. I was slowly regaining consciousness but was not alert enough to follow commands.

"Nope, he's not responding," she said.

"Look, his eyes are blinking," I heard William's familiar voice in the distance.

"That's a good sign. We turned his sedation down. Let's give him some time and see how he does without it."

I felt severe pain in my abdomen. I grimaced trying to get into a more comfortable position. I tried to lift my arm to grab my stomach, but it was tied to the bed rail. I tried to talk but there was a tube in my throat. I tried to cough it up but all I could do was choke.

"Easy now, easy," William tried to calm me down.

I was confused. *What's happening? Where's my mom? Where's John? Are they okay?* I started to cry. I thought about Nathaniel. *Where's he? Is he going to come after me and finish me off in the hospital? Did they even know it was him who did this?* I wanted to give my statement to the cops immediately so that he could be arrested and prosecuted. I had to take the tube out of my mouth so they could hear my testimony. I tried to move my hand towards the tube but was unsuccessful in overcoming the restraints.

"Easy, easy," William continued. "You're safe now."

"He's breathing over the machine and following directions. Shall we try to take the tube out?" an unfamiliar male voice in the distance spoke. "Okay."

A doctor came over to me. He was smiling. He pressed some buttons on the equipment next to me. Then he and some nurses removed tape around my mouth. "Okay, James, go ahead and cough. Cough it up. Good," he said as I followed his instructions. I was still afraid and confused, then I felt Williams hand grab mine and it gave me the comfort I needed.

"Where's mom?" I asked in a hoarse voice. No one responded. They looked at each other spooked and then looked at William who immediately started crying. They didn't have to say anything. I knew from their look that my mom had died.

"John?" I asked.

"James," William spoke, "Your mom and John, they didn't make it."

I wept loudly. There was empathy on the doctor and nurse's faces. They held each other and William held me. "I am so sorry," he said.

"My dad! It was my dad who did it."

"We know. The police followed Nathaniel into an abandoned building. Before they could arrest him, he killed himself."

I had so many feelings. There was anger, pain, grief, and fear. Knowing the murderer of my family was dead was comforting. Knowing the murderer was family was disturbing. I tried to sit up to avoid drowning in my tears but contracting my stomach muscles caused worsening pain. William and the nurse helped me to get comfortable. I touched my bandaged abdomen.

"You suffered two gunshot wounds," the doctor informed me. "They both were to the back with exit wounds in the abdomen. You have been here for two weeks. We have done three surgeries to repair as much as we can..." He continued talking about my injuries and prognosis, but I failed to hear him as I was still stuck on being the only survivor of my entire family.

"Who's going to take care of me?" I spoke directly to William interrupting the doctor.

William opened his mouth but couldn't get the words out then he left out the room. His absence hurt even more.

"A social worker assigned to your case has arranged for your grandmother to take you in."

"Grandmother?" I didn't know my mother's parents. They kicked her out when she was pregnant with me. And my father's parents were both dead.

"Yes, Adaline Claytor. She is your mother's mom."

"Adaline? But I don't even know her. She doesn't even want me. Can't I just go with William?"

The nurse and doctor looked at each other then back at me. "I'm sorry, but William declined adopting you. Your grandmother agreed to take you in."

Declined? My mind couldn't grasp why he, the only remaining family I knew would decline taking me in. Anger became my dominant emotion.

A few days later, Adaline Claytor walked into my hospital room. She had an exaggerated southern drawl. "Hi James, I'm your grandma! Well aren't you just a handsome little thing. You look'n just like your grandpa. Of course, he's gone to glory now, God rest his soul. Passed away about seven years ago."

I didn't speak to her. I folded my arms across my chest and looked out the window. Where was she for the first thirteen years of my life? Why did she abandon my mother at the times when she needed her the most? She was that mad about my birth that she stopped talking to her only daughter? That told me all I needed to know about Mrs. Adaline Claytor. I was not loved by her. I was not wanted by her. And I didn't want to be with her.

My lack of enthusiasm about her presence didn't stop her from trying though. She showed up to my room every day and talked with me. It was mostly small talk. She'd ask me how my day went and how I was feeling. I'd ignore her. She'd talk about the weather and the room she had prepared for me back at her house in North Carolina. I'd ignore her. But after a while, I started to respect her persistence. It was more than what William had done. He stopped visiting me about a week after I was extubated. I guess he grew tired of me asking him why he wouldn't adopt me.

The next few months were an arduous road to recovery. One of the bullets nicked my kidney, so I pissed blood for weeks. The other bullet nicked a nerve near my spinal cord that affected my right leg. I went through lots of physical therapy to be able to compensate for that loss. Both bullets went through my intestines. The surgeons had to remove several feet of damaged gut. My food was hard to digest but overtime I learned what I could eat and what elicited more pain. Both bullets left disfiguring scars on my abdomen. I was grieved by the look of it. *I'll never be able to get a six pack. I'll never be able to take my shirt off in public without stares from onlookers. What about the beach? Swimming pool? Could I no longer participate in those beloved activities? If I did, would I have to cover my scars.*

I went home with Adaline. She had a nice house in a rural area. It was nothing like I was used to. She loved going to church. I hated it. I was mad at God. If He was so loving, why did he allow all this to happen to me? He was supposed to be my rock and my shield. But where was He when my family was murdered? I'd sit in church with my arms folded and a scowl on my face. Everything the preacher said sounded like a crock of shit. I blocked every word from taking root in my heart. I blocked every person who tried to get close to me.

Then Chloe called. It was easy to block those I didn't know. It was even easier to block those who had hurt me. But Chloe was neither. She was already deeply rooted in my heart and she was hurting right along with me.

"Hey," she said.

"Hey," I responded holding back tears.

"I miss you."

"I miss you too."

"I miss Bianca. She was the only mother I knew. I miss John, he was a brother to me same as you."

"Me too," I couldn't put up a hard front anymore. My walls crumbled and I cried. I thought crying was weakness. I thought it would make the pain hurt more. But instead, it was cleansing.

After that, Chloe and I talked at least once a week. We helped each other grow through our pain. We were not blood related, and we lived in different states. But she was the only family I had left. She was my sister for life.

Chapter 15 – William's Frost in 2018

"Jeremy was not a match," I cried as I shared the news with James.

"It's okay, we'll find the guy who did this," he responded as he rubbed my shoulder. Despite all that he had been through, he still grew up to be a proper young man. I was proud of him and I regretted my role, more accurately lack thereof, in his life.

"I should have been there for you. Seven years ago. You needed me. I…I… should have been there. It's just that…"

"I know. I understand. My mom's death took a toll on all of us."

"That's no excuse. I should have been there. I was so engulfed in my own misery I wasn't there to help you with yours. And you…you remind me so much of your mother. Your eyes, your spunk, your strength…I just couldn't handle…I apologize with all my heart."

"All is forgiven," he said squeezing my shoulder harder. I grabbed his hand and squeezed back.

"I haven't been to church since then," I admitted.

He nodded. "I stopped going too. My grandma tried to make me go but I was not having it. I gave her such a hard time."

"Really? I remember you used to love church. Remember your solos in the choir? Bianca was so proud."

He giggled at the memory. "Yeah, I remember. Church just wasn't the same without her. I do miss it though. Sometimes I feel like God is calling me back. Especially times like these when it seems like everything is going wrong. You know? Times when you know you need a miracle."

"Maybe we should go…together," I suggested.

"I'd like that."

**

We walked into New Life Christian Church just as the choir was winding down, and Pastor Charles took the podium to speak. It felt weird walking through those doors again. I remembered seeing Bianca, James, and John for the first time. The spot where she broke down and cried was a few yards in front of me. The pew where I stood when Pastor announced our engagement was to my left. The pew where I sat for Bianca and John's funeral was to my right. I wanted to turn and run, but James warmly grasped my shoulder, and I knew I could continue.

"Oh my God," Pastor Charles stated when James and I walked into the sanctuary. I smiled and waved. "It's William and James. Church, let's welcome our brothers in the faith back home." Immediately old friendly faces approached with smiles. They gave us handshakes, hugs, and salutations. With each greeting, my unease faded until there was no nervousness remaining.

"Well, as most of you know I lost my beloved wife of thirty-two years to cancer five months ago." I had no idea that First Lady Grace had passed. She was a delightful woman. Always willing to help. She was the shoulder I cried on at the funeral. I felt bad not being there when Pastor went through losing her.

Pastor continued, "I thought todays sermon was for me. But now I realize, it was for someone else." He looked straight at me. "Ain't it funny how God works sometimes. He knows exactly where you are going to be and when. He knows exactly what you need, and He provides. It is not by coincidence that you are here today. Church please turn your Bibles to Daniel 3:8-29."

It was one of my favorite Bible stories. The story of Shadrach, Meshach, and Abednego, three Israelites who refused to worship an idol god even though the king who ruled over them sanctioned a law stating if they did not worship, they would be thrown into a fire. When it was discovered that these boys refused to worship, they were threatened with death, they responded, "If this be so, our God whom we serve is able to deliver us from the burning fiery furnace, and he will deliver us out of your hand, O king. But if not, be it known to you, O king, that we will not serve your gods or worship the golden image that you have set up (Daniel 3:17-18 ESV)."

"You see," Pastor Charles said, "these boys knew that God was able to deliver them if it was in His will. But they also realized that God is not a genie. He doesn't answer all prayers. However, they were still willing to serve, follow, and praise God weather he answered their prayers or not. I remember when my wife was diagnosed with colon cancer. I remember the surgeries, and the radiation. I remember restless nights of Grace moaning in pain and vomiting in the bathroom. I watched helplessly as she wasted away.

I prayed a lot in those times. Despite my prayers, she continued to deteriorate. I stood by and witnessed other people's prayers miraculously getting answered. Other people's marriages were saved, other people were delivered from debt, others were cured. But my prayers went unanswered. Loosing Grace was the hardest thing I ever had to go through. John 5:24 says 'Truly, truly, I say to you, whoever hears my word and believes Him who sent me has eternal life. He does not come into judgment but has passed from death to life.' You see, her physical body may be gone and buried, but her spirit lives on forever because she believed. I am comforted because I know Grace is no longer in pain, she no longer has tears, and she no longer suffers. It was in God's will for her to live with Him in Heaven. Just like it was in God's will that Shadrach, Meshach, and Abednego lived. They still had to go through the fire though. They still had to suffer. Sometimes God will answer our prayers but not the way we want. See they prayed that they wouldn't have to go through the fire at all. They prayed they'd be removed from under Nebuchadnezzar's rules, laws, and punishments all together. But it didn't happen the way they thought it would. They still were thrown into the fire, just like sometimes we must suffer through whatever fiery trials come our way. But when they were in the fire, they were not alone. Look in the text. It says when King Nebuchadnezzar looked in the furnace, he saw not three men but four. God was with them. God is with you when you are struggling. You are not alone. God was with Grace and I during the diagnosis, the treatments, and the sleepless nights. He was there comforting us, helping us, and shielding our hearts from getting burnt. I was not alone when Grace passed. You were not alone when your friend, or your fiancé, or your mother passed, God was there with you. He was always there. And yes, God allowed your suffering. But He did it for a good reason. Look back at the scripture. Because Babylon witnessed these three boys survive the unsurvivable, Babylon was converted to believing in God. These Israelite boys' suffering saved a nation. Same with my Grace. Since her death, we have started our hospice ministry in her honor. We reach out to families who too are going through the toiling trials of watching a loved one transition. Because of Grace's death, we have helped seventeen families so far with spiritual guidance, funeral arrangements, counseling, and other bereavement services. We have saved nine people through that ministry, one of which died only two days after he was saved. There is bigger. There is better. Grace is better than ever and so is our church and all it took was a little suffering. Only a short period in the fiery furnace. I never thought I'd be able to live without my Grace. I envisioned her death as unsurvivable for me. But I survived the unsurvivable and you can too. Not only can you survive but that stressing can turn into a blessing."

I held back tears in my eyes. But when I looked over at James and tears flowed freely from his, I couldn't help but let my pain flow too. My heart was filled with not just the message but with Pastor Charles' strength through the loss of his wife. I felt guilt that through the death of Bianca, my heart turned cold. I avoided any situation where love could bloom. I rejected everything that reminded me of Bianca. I lost faith that God was good.

I thought that God was good because he answered prayers. But that was wrong. Sometimes God does not answer prayers. It's not because he doesn't love us. It's not because he doesn't want what is best for us. It's not because he is not almighty. It is not because God is not good. It's because sometimes He has bigger and better plans than what we could even imagine.

When Bianca died, I focused all my effort into work and Chloe. My focus on work paved the way to me becoming a judge. My effort into Chloe took a broken girl who wouldn't talk to a straight A student destined for greatness. Granted, her assault was a setback. But I had to have faith that whatever the outcome, it would all work out for our good.

During alter call, James, and I both went to the front of the church. Church members gathered around us as Pastor Charles prayed for the healing of our hearts, prayed for our current trials, and prayed for our future spiritual restoration. I didn't realize how much I missed fellowship until that moment. Their prayers were like medicine for my soul.

After service, there were refreshments being served in the multipurpose room. "Can we go?" James asked, "I'm starved."

"Sure," I responded and upon entering the hall Pastor Charles approached me with haste.

"Brother William, it is so good to see you. What brings you this way? Last I heard you took a job as a judge in King George."

"Um, yes. I uh, haven't been to church in a while. You know…"

"Yes, I do. I understand now more than ever. But I am so glad to see you back. How's that lovely daughter of yours?"

"Chloe, she's…uh…she's…"

"She's not doing well," James finished.

"Oh no, what's wrong?"

"She's been in the hospital for the last couple of months. Drug overdose, they say but..." I tried to hold back the tears as I spoke.

"Chloe is a wonderful girl. I am so sorry to hear that she is going through a rough time. We will definitely keep her lifted up in prayer. And you should pray too."

"But…why? Why should I pray? What if God doesn't hear that prayer either?"

Pastor knowingly nodded his head. "That doesn't mean we don't pray. Let your petition be known to God. Sometimes He shakes our world because he wants to get our attention. Sometimes all He's waiting for is for us to go to Him. He hears you. Things will work out."

Chapter 16 – Cadence's Frost in 2018

There was so much guilt built up in my heart. Chloe was in the ICU and it was all my fault. If I hadn't been so wrapped up in my own affairs, she would not have been hurt. I had been contemplating coming out of the closet for years. But I was afraid. What would other's think of me? What would my family do? What about church? What about God?

When Jamie came to school, I knew she was keeping the same secret I had been holding in. I'm not sure how I knew. Maybe it was the way she looked at me, or the way she carried herself, but something identified her as a lesbian. I had been too afraid to approach. Then Chloe encouraged me to be myself. Chloe loved me no matter what. Knowing that I had her support made me feel more accepted and slightly eased the fear of revealing my truth to the world. And so, I took a step out on faith and asked Jamie out on a date. When she agreed, I was beside myself.

Our first date we had dinner at a little hole in the wall diner. We both decided to go to a place where no one would notice us. We didn't want rumors to circulate before our relationship even started. The conversation was nice. She was further along in the process of being public than I. She had already told her mother who was supportive. They were strategically planning to tell her close-minded father.

With me, the only person who knew was Chloe. I was still working on accepting myself. I wasn't sure what I'd do if others didn't accept me. At the end of our date, standing in the parking lot at my car, we had our first kiss. I had kissed boys before, but there was no thrill in it. With Jamie, there was. I felt the butterflies build up in my chest and the passion overflow in my gut.

"You going to Jeremy's party next weekend?" she asked.

"Umm…" I wanted to go but I thought of Chloe. I knew she needed me. Realizing that Maybeline had died really sent her into a deep depression. I wasn't sure if she'd be in the mood to party and I didn't want to leave her alone on a Saturday night.

"I'll be there," Jamie said as she twirled her hair and seduced me with her beautiful brown eyes.

"In that case, I'll be there too!" She smiled harder and gave me a peck on the lips then we parted ways.

Chloe didn't want to go, but I convinced her that it would be good for her. She went for me. And the entire time, I was engaged in flirtatious conversation with Jamie while she was sitting on the couch looking bored. She persistently ignored advances of various young men trying to get with her and declined spiked drinks that were offered.

"Come to the car with me," Jamie whispered in my ear.

"For what?"

Jamie suggestively shimmied her C cups. I smiled.

"Hey Chloe!" I shouted, "you mind if I..."

Chloe playfully brushed me away. "Go ahead. I'll be fine. Besides, I got Joshie here to keep me company." She winked at him. It was one of the few times in high school that Joshua came out of his shell and made an appearance at a social event. He was in an adjacent chair watching over our conversation and taking sips from a red plastic cup, I figured he had juice in there since he never drank. He raised his cup to me confirming that he'd watch over her which made me feel a little better about leaving her.

"Okay!" I kissed Chloe on the cheek. "Love you!"

"Yeah, yeah! Behave yourself," she winked.

I sat in the back of Jamie's car making out while my best friend was experiencing the worst moment of her life. Our passionate session was interrupted by the flashing of police lights who pulled up to break up the party.

"Oh shit!" Jamie said. "We gotta go." Jamie hoped in the front seat and started her engine.

"I can't, Chloe's still in there."

"Shit! Call her. Tell her to meet us on Main Street."

I took out my cell phone and called as Jamie drove off. Voicemail. I called again. Voicemail.

"She's not answering. Turn around," I demanded Jamie.

"Hell no. I've been drinking. I am not going to jail today. My parents will kill me. Let's just lay low for a few hours then go back and get her. I'm sure she'll be fine. Besides Joshua is with her. She's good."

"I guess," I responded but I was worried. Jamie tried to start kissing on me again, but I was too engulfed in concern for Chloe's well-being that I couldn't engage.

"You still thinking of Chloe?" Jamie noticed my decreased interest. "She's fine. Damn."

I rolled my eyes, got out of the car, and started walking to my car.

"Babe!" Jamie yelled from her window. "I'm sorry. I didn't mean it like that." I kept walking. "It's a long walk back to Jeremy's house." I kept walking. "Okay, fine fine. Get back in, I'll take you over there." I stopped and got back in the car. When we pulled up to the house, the place was crawling with cops. Jamie slowed down and cased the area before she let me out about a block away.

"You sure you want to go in there?"

"I have to make sure Chloe's okay."

"I get it. I do but..." She recognized my determination and decided not to argue. "Nevermind. Can I call you tomorrow?"

"Mmm hmm," I agreed. Jamie blew me a kiss then took off.

I prayed as I walked to the house, then I got a text message from Jeremy.

"They took Chloe to the hospital."

"OMG! Which one?"

There was no answer. I ran toward the house to try to get more information. As I stepped onto his yard, I saw the cops escorting him in handcuffs. He looked at me as he passed. His eyes spoke clearly, "I'm fine. Go check on Chloe."

There are two hospitals in our area. I called them both and found out she had been sent to Spotsy Regional.

**

Two months later, there was little progress in her condition. James, William, and I had been consumed with finding out what happened those three hours between the time I left her and the time she ended up in the ER. I was laying on my bed in my bedroom trying to figure out who I knew that could trace the message on Joshua's phone when I heard a tap on my window. I sat up and looked at the window but didn't see anything. *Must be my imagination*, I thought. Then I heard another tap. This one was louder. I ran to my window and standing in my driveway was Jamie who had been hurling rocks at my pane trying to get my attention. I opened the window.

"Jamie!" I loudly whispered, "What are you doing here?"

"I missed you!"

I motioned for her to go over to the side door. I met her there and snuck her up to my room. Once in my room I gave her a big hug and kiss.

"You haven't called me in a while. Are we still cool?" she asked.

"Yeah, of course. I've just been busy, you know. Chloe in the ICU. Daniel just getting out of rehab. Between that and school, I guess I just…you know what? There's no excuse. I should have called you. I am sorry for that. But I am glad you're here."

"I'm glad too," she smiled, and we started kissing again. I was distracted. I needed to find someone who could trace the video back to the source.

"What's wrong?"

"Nothing," I tried to kiss her again.

"No, I know you better than that. Something's on your mind. What's up?"

"It's Chloe," I confessed.

Jamie sighed then straightened trying to be supportive. "Look, I know she's your best friend, and she's in the hospital, but what happens to her now is out of your control. She decided to take a bunch of drugs she wasn't used to and she's in the hospital because of her decision."

I angrily walked away from Jamie, "But maybe she didn't willingly take drugs. Maybe she was drugged."

"By whom exactly?"

"Joshua was sent a video the night Chloe overdosed. It was edited, but I think the full version may give us insight into what really happened that night."

"So, you need someone to trace the video back to the source?"

"Yes!"

"That's easy. You know my girl Tonya, she's a genius when it comes to hacking devices. She got you. Just send the message to me and we'll find the source."

"Seriously!"

"Yeah!"

I was so happy. I hugged Jamie around the neck and kissed her repeatedly. The cute pecks I placed on her face turned into lustful tongue lashings. She followed me to my bed where the passion continued. She took off my shirt and I unbuttoned her pants.

We kissed, rubbed, and groped harder. Then my bedroom door opened, and Daniel walked in, "Cadence have you seen my…Oh my God! Cadence! What the fuck are you doing?" He tried to cover his eyes but couldn't help but look at us as we scrambled to put our clothes back on.

Jamie ran out the room in embarrassment. "Daniel! Don't you know how to knock!" I yelled as I chased after Jamie. I was too slow. As I made my way to the front door she was already taking off in her car. "Damn it!" I shouted as I saw her car sped down the street.

I stomped into the house determined to give Daniel a piece of my mind, but he started fussing at me before I could say anything.

"Cadence, what the fuck was that? You're experimenting with girls now?"

"It's not an experiment Daniel! I'm a lesbian!"

"A lesbian! How can you be a lesbian and be so into church?"

"The same way you can be a drug addict and be in church."

"It's not the same," he replied with a condescending tone.

"You're right! It's not the same. You had a choice to start drugs. I didn't. I was born this way."

He scoffed, "Born? Born? No, people don't come out the womb talking bout I want to fuck another girl. That was your choice."

I buried my face in my hands. It was all I could do to keep from slapping the shit out of him. I was so angry. He had no idea of what I had been through all my life. He had no idea of what I felt. I am a Christian. I love God. I love Jesus. I believe Jesus is my Lord and Savior. But I am also attracted to women. Both being a Christian and being a lesbian is who I am.

"Does dad know?" he asked.

Oh Shit! I was so angry at Daniel I didn't even think about dad. I was nowhere near ready to face my dad's criticism. "Daniel, please don't tell him."

Daniel looked at me with a sinister grin on his face.

"Daniel, please! Please!" Cadence pleaded.

"Mmm, okay. I won't tell him. But you are going to have to tell him sooner or later."

"I know! I know!" I responded but hoped that day would never come. Daniel walked away still grinning.

Over the next two weeks, Jamie and I grew closer and more in love. In the past I tried to fake an attraction to boys I was dating but nothing materialized because deep down, that wasn't me. With Jamie, no front was needed. My desire for her came naturally.

"I love you," she whispered to me one day in the lunchroom. It was exciting for me to hear. For the first time I felt like my desire to find true love, get married, and start a family was possible. I kissed her and whispered, "Love you too."

She handed me a piece of paper with a number on it.

"What's this?"

"It's the source. That's the number the message that was sent to Joshua originated from. It took a while, but we got it."

"What!?" I kissed her again.

"Alright, break it up you two," Mr. Roberts, the algebra teacher who had cafeteria duty that week told us.

"You know it's real funny how Tori and Brandon can make out all day every day," Jamie said pointing to that happy heterosexual couple. "But when it comes to a same sex couple you want to break it up."

"None of you adolescents should be kissing each other. Especially not you two."

Jamie rolled her eyes unmoved. I couldn't help but feel a sting from his words.

I dialed the number on my phone and discovered that the number was linked to a contact that was already in my phone, Jeremy.

"Oh God, it's Jeremy's phone. But how could that be? He was in jail when the message was sent. Plus, he already said he didn't know about the message."

"Well who had access to Jeremy's phone?"

"Shoot, everyone at the party. That was like half the school."

"Well what about after the party? Everyone left when Jeremy got arrested. Everyone except…"

"Anna!" we simultaneously shouted as we both remembered that Jeremey's girlfriend was the only other person in the house either than Chloe when the ambulance was called. Anna didn't share the same lunch period we had but I planned to approach her after school.

I ran out of my last period class as soon as the bell rang and stood by Anna's locker. "Anna!" I shouted when I saw her approach.

She looked at me startled. "You know anything about this?" I held up the video so she could see.

"Yes, I sent that video to Joshua's phone."

"Why?"

"Jeremy got locked up for Chloe's drug overdose. But it wasn't Jeremy who gave her the drugs."

"So what? You're saying it was Michael? That's why you sent the video? So, Joshua would have evidence against Michael?"

"It wasn't Michael either. I sent the video to Joshua hoping it would prompt him to confess."

"Confess? Confess what?"

"Confess that he was the one who drugged Chloe."

"You're full of shit! You're just trying to blame this on Joshua so you can get Jeremy out of jail." I argued. There was no way our close friend - skinny, nerdy, never-do-wrong, scared of his own shadow Joshua could have done anything to hurt Chloe.

"No really. Joshua must have edited that video. Here's the real one." Anna dug her cell phone out of her locker and scrolled to the video. The first few minutes were identical to Joshua's video. Teenagers drinking and partying. Michael and Chloe arguing in the background. Michael pulling Chloe into the room. Then more wild teenagers yelling and dancing in the camera. Then, the door opens and a frustrated Michael storms out. Only two minutes had lapsed from them going in and him coming out. It wasn't enough time for a drugging or a rape. Joshua had been sitting in the same chair where I had left him when I ran away with Jamie. His expression was angry, and he had been staring at the door sipping from his red cup for the entire two minutes. When Michael left, Joshua stood up, grabbed a beer, grabbed a handful of pills from a bowl on the side table, popped half in his mouth, and put the other half in the drink. Then he walked into the room where Chloe remained.

"What the fuck?" I said shocked.

"Wait, there's more," Anna said as she scrolled to another section on her phone. "This is video downloaded from Jeremy's security camera at his backdoor. It showed a shirtless Joshua run out in fear. He scrambled to put on his shirt as he ran. Anna pointed out that the time between the end of the cell phone video and the beginning of the security camera's feed was exactly forty-seven minutes.

I was still suspicious, "Why didn't you send this to the police?"

"My mother works for Joshua's dad. She's a single mom and she is all I have. She needs that job. If they knew I was the only witness to this crime, my mom's job would be threatened for sure. And where would that leave me? The only way I knew the truth could come out without my family suffering was if Joshua confessed. I was hoping the video would guilt him into it. But I guess I was wrong."

I tried to hide my shock, "Can you send those videos to me?"

"Sure thing."

I jumped in my car and sped towards the hospital still holding back my tears. As soon as I got to the parking lot, I screamed cried and yelled. *How could this be? I trusted Joshua. We trusted Joshua. How could he do this to her?*

I angrily hustled into Chloe's room where James was calmly reading the Bible to her.

"Cadence!" he said looking happier than usual to see me. Hi demeaner changed at the sight of my disturbed face, "You okay?"

"No!"

"What's wrong?"

I handed him my phone and showed him the original video. I paced back and forth in the room staring at James' face while it turned from serene to rage. "That little shit!" he said. He got up grabbed his phone and called William.

"Hey! Where you at?"

William was outside in the waiting room. He asked for James and me to meet him out there before giving James a chance to let him know what we discovered. We went figuring it would be best to tell William in person. When we got to the waiting room, there was a crowd waiting for us. Pastor Charles, Dr. Brown, Daniel, my dad, and a few folks from our church were huddled around trying to comfort William.

"Dad! What are you doing here? What's going on?" I asked worried that Chloe's condition had worsened, and they were getting ready to inform us.

"Nothing sweetheart," he leaned over and kissed my forehead. "William just asked us to come and pray for Chloe."

Pastor Charles started, "Come, let's all join hands there is power in numbers."

"Excuse me Pastor," Daniel raised his hand. "Is that power diminished when there's a lesbian praying with you?" Then he looked at me with a smirk. I turned bright red. William and Pastor Charles both raised one eyebrow. My dad furrowed his eyebrows and looked at me suspiciously.

"If you are asking if God hears a sinner's prayer, the answer is yes," Pastor answered. "If God didn't hear sinners' prayers then none of us would be able to speak to Him as we are all sinners. Now, shall we continue? Please, bow your heads. Heavenly Father…" Pastor Charles must have said a spirit filled prayer because I heard a lot of "Yes Lord" and "Amen" from the group. But I didn't hear a word of it because I was appalled at what Daniel said.

"What was that?" I asked Daniel in private after the prayer session adjourned.

"What was what?" he tried to play innocent.

"You know what."

"That was me trying to save your soul. I love you sis, but I hate what you are doing. It's not right and if you don't stop, you're going straight to hell." He pushed by me. I was so hot you could have cooked an egg on my forehead.

James approached me. "Hey you okay?" he asked.

"Yeah."

"Cool, I told William about Joshua. We are headed to the police station now. You good staying here with Chloe?"

"Yeah." I figured that sitting with Chloe would help me calm down.

"Bet!" he said then they marched off together.

I spent my night talking to Chloe. I missed her being able to talk back to me. She was always understanding, gave the best advice, and made me smile when I felt down. I got a phone call from James around midnight, "Hey, they got a warrant to obtain Joshua's DNA. They are going to his house to serve him tomorrow afternoon. It's only a matter of time for justice to be served."

Chapter 17 – Joshua's Seasons

I was born into money. My dad is the CEO of a successful real estate company. My mom, a supportive homemaker, strived to make our life comfortable. Homemade family meals, organizing social gatherings, Homeowners Association Meetings, and active PTA membership was her thing. I was an only child so they both poured into me. And I strived to make my family proud by doing good in school and staying out of trouble. From the outside looking in, we were the perfect family living the great American Dream. But inside the walls of our home, there was a different story. My dad was an avid adulterer. His years of repeated infidelity ripped holes through our family unit. Initially he tried to keep his many mistresses secret. Mom would always find out. She'd get hurt and mad, but she never left. She was so dedicated that after a while, my dad stopped trying to hide his affairs. He knew she wasn't going anywhere, and he grew comfortable in his destructive ways.

My mom coped with it unhealthily. When my dad wondered into the house in the middle of the night disheveled with lipstick stains and the scent of another woman, she never confronted him. In public, she kept a plastered smile on her face and continued to support him. Instead of addressing the problem, she ate a lot, drank a lot, and dedicated her life to raising me. She did not hide her disdain for my dad from me. She'd often mention her hatred of him and the women he cheated with. Bitch, ho, cunt, gigolo, prostitute were all names I was familiar with in childhood because my mom repeated it so much when referencing her husband and his lovers. She was a very passive aggressive woman and would often scheme to get these women fired from their jobs or ostracized from their friends and family. She wrote several letters to the bosses of dad's lovers pretending to be a customer unhappy with the woman's service. She'd make anonymous phone calls to the husbands of women she thought were sleeping with her husband and declare the alleged affair which resulted in several divorces. She'd spread rumors about these women, some true and some not, at community meetings or on social media. She was successful in her schemes, and she felt comfort in punishing people for their crimes against her.

Neither parent knew what impact their poor decisions had on my psyche. I was taught by one that cheating was okay as long as you get away with it. I was taught by the other to be vengeful passive-aggressively. I was taught by both that the world is cruel, lying is okay, and people will hurt you without regret or consequence. Thus, I decided at a young age to shut the world out. I lived life with my head down. I had no interest in people because I had no desire to get hurt. The only thing I trusted were numbers. Numbers were straight forward, honest, and universal. I poured myself into school, namely math. My mom loved my passion for arithmetic. My dad wished I were more athletic and social. He voiced his disdain for my nerdy demeanor often. But I ignored him. My walls were built up too thick for him to penetrate.

But all that changed the first day of high school, when Chloe walked into gym class. Just one look at her and the stony protection around my heart was compromised. She had the most beautiful chocolate skin I had ever encountered, and her perfect smile sent shivers down my spine. She looked around at all the faces of our classmates searching for a friend. When she looked at me, my heart dropped into my pelvis and I smiled nervously in return. *Oh my God, Oh my God, she's walking over to me. What do I do? What do I say?* I thought as she approached me.

"Hi! I'm Chloe."

"Uhhh…."*speak God-dammit* "…I'm Joshua."

"Joshua, Josh, Joshie. Nice to meet you."

I didn't say anything to her for the rest of gym class, nor when I saw her the next day. On day number three, Chloe, and Cadence both invited me to sit with them at lunch. I was too shocked to smile, but I gladly accepted the invite. They were both really cool and we all became close. But I continued to hide behind my wall. I never told Chloe how I felt about her. It was painful to hear her talk about other guys she had crushes on. It was more painful to hear her talk about how unworthy she thought she was of dating any of those guys. Because I didn't want my true feelings exposed, I restrained from telling her that I thought she was a ten, and any of those guys would be fortunate to have her on their arm. I knew that if I said it, she'd end up with them and I'd end up hurt. I didn't want her to end up with those dirtbags who I knew were only interested in cheap thrills and quick entanglements. I wanted so much more with her. I wanted love, peace, and happiness. I wanted a future with her. But I was stuck in a role as her nerdy side kick.

Summer of 2018, I had enough. Three years of torturing myself, sitting next to Chloe in the lunchroom, and hiding my love for her drove me wild. I made the decision to climb out of my hole and risk heartbreak. I drove to her house, dressed in a suit and tie, with 12 long stem red roses. But I was too late. I saw Michael's car parked in her driveway. *Maybe they are just friends,* I tried to comfort myself as I got out of my car. But as I approached the front door, I heard the sensual moans escaping her bedroom window. Crushed, I retreated back to my fortress.

Chloe still called me occasionally to chat as friends. I was standoffish. She never mentioned Michael and I never asked. The summer concluded and autumn came.

Cadence approached me in the hallway at class one Friday. "You going to Jeremey's party tonight?" she asked.

"You know I don't go to parties."

"Yeah, but I need you to go to this one."

"Why?"

"Because I'm worried about Chloe." I raised my eyebrow curiously waiting for Cadence to continue. "She's been acting strange all school year. You haven't noticed?"

"Yeah, but what does that have to do with me going to a party?"

"Well, I want to go because Jamie is going to be there. But I don't want Chloe to be alone so…"

"So, you want me to hang out with Chloe while you go get all flirty with Ms. Jamie."

"Yes."

I looked at Cadence skeptically.

"Please Joshie!"

I couldn't resist. Chloe made up that nickname for me and I caved whenever either one of them called me it. I pretended like I hated the name, but they knew otherwise.

"Okay fine, but you owe me."

"Yay! Thank you Joshie! This will be so much fun! You won't regret it." Cadence jumped up and down, kissed me on the cheek, then walked away.

I regretted the decision soon after I walked into Jeremey's house. Chloe was there, looking beautiful as ever, but she had a sadness to her. I filled a red cup with liquid courage and sipped pumping myself up to approach her. I watched her as I sipped, and I rehearsed what I was going to say to her in my head. *Chloe, I want you. I've always wanted you. I want you to be my friend, my lover, my girlfriend, and one day my wife. I want to be the one that fills your life with joy. I want to be the man you've always deserved.* Cadence left and my buzz intensified. It was the perfect moment to make my move. I stood up and initiated the walk to my destiny when Michael entered, breezed by me, and started talking to Chloe.

"You didn't do it?" he fussed.

She tried to discretely whisper, "What the hell are you doing here?"

"My dad called me, told me you stood him up."

"I couldn't go through with it. It was just too…"

"I told you I can't do this shit!"

"And I can't…" Chloe was getting angry. She paused and took a breath to recoup.

"You need to get rid of it!" Michael yelled as he grabbed her arm and began to pull her away. "I'm here to make sure you go through with it this time."

"No!" Chloe yanked her arm back. Michael grabbed her again and dragged her into a back room.

I sat back in my chair, sipping on more vodka, and staring at the door they closed behind them. I wondered if I should go rescue her. I could go in there, beat Michael's ass, and she'd romantically fall into my arms. No way I could do that. Michael was one of the jocks. Lacrosse, baseball, swimming, and soccer were his thing. He played one sport for each season. And I was an all year long math whiz who had never been in a fight. I tried to come up with a better plan. I knew I could use my brains to defeat his brawn. But how?

Then the door opened, and an irritated Michael stormed out grabbing a beer on his way. I stood up. This was my chance. I grabbed a beer then grabbed a handful of recreational drugs that were on the table. I popped most in my mouth and a few in my beer. It gave me the confidence to walk into the room.

"Hey!" Chloe said as she saw me. She laid on the bed. I could tell she had been crying. She wiped her tears away and smiled. She held up a tray of marijuana and pills. "I found Jeremey's stash." She took a handful and swallowed.

"Chloe, I…"

"Shhhh. Close the door," she suggestively whispered. I complied. Her hips swayed seductively as she strolled my way. I was frozen in my tracks. She wrapped her arm across my shoulder and looked me in the eye. There was a grin on her face. Then she took the beer from my grasp and chugged on it.

"Chloe there's…"

"Shhh," she cut me off preventing me from telling her there were additional drugs in the beer. "I know what I'm doing," she whispered then she passionately kissed me. Initially, I pulled away thinking, *she's drunk. She doesn't know what she is doing. I don't want our first time to be like this.* Then I figured, *wait a minute. She's not drunk yet. I watched her the entire party, and she didn't engage in any drinking or drugs until after she came in this room a few minutes ago. The drugs she just ingested hasn't kicked in yet. She does know what she is doing. And she wants me.* I had been waiting for that moment for years and I wasn't going to let it pass me by. I kissed her back more passionately. I grabbed her voluptuous butt and lifted her. She wrapped her legs around my waist and continued her embrace. I lowered her onto the bed. She ripped off my clothes, I ripped off hers, and I enthusiastically made love to her mind, body, and soul. I marveled at the enticing sounds she groaned as I went deeper and deeper into her abyss. I tried to fill every part of her with my love. I tried to take away every pain that she ever endured and replace it with joy. Her arched back and trembling legs as she climaxed let me know that my mission was accomplished. I allowed myself to explode in her then I collapsed. She took all my energy and reserve. The high from our orgasm plus the high from the many drugs in my system rendered me unconscious.

I'm not sure how long I was out but when I woke, I was still on top of her, and she was unresponsive. There was vomitus dripping from her lips. Her eyes were opened and fixed.

"Chloe! Chloe!" I shook her and yelled in attempt to arouse her. I leaned over her mouth to see if she was breathing, but I didn't hear her gasp. I got up promptly and looked around the room in a panic. I knew what it looked like - dead girl, drugs, and me naked with her in the room. Rape and murder – it would be an opened and shut case. All I could think to do is what my parents taught me. Lie, cheat, manipulate – do what you can to not get caught. I had been invisible to my peers my entire life. I hoped that my invisibility would be of advantage in my time of need. I figured no one noticed me, the nerdy math genius, go into this room nor leave. I figured no one would suspect me, the stand-up quiet kid. I could easily fade into the background. I grabbed my clothes and ran out the backdoor without saying a word.

Two hours later, I got a text from an unknown number with the video. There was an associated text, "I won't tell as long as you get Jeremy out of jail." I figured Jeremy was being charged with Chloe's murder. My confession was needed to get him out. But I couldn't do that. I had to figure out a better way.

My phone rang. It was Cadence. I couldn't answer the phone. But she called again and again. Then texted. I knew if I didn't answer she'd be suspicious. I picked up the phone having no clue what I would say to her to cover my tracks.

"Chloe's in the hospital!" she fussed.

"What? What happened? Is she okay?" I thought she was dead but maybe there was a chance she'd survive.

"I don't know. You were supposed to be watching her. You tell me what happened."

"I…uh…I…I saw Michael. He showed up and they started arguing. Then they went into a room alone. That's all I know?"

"Michael? Michael Harris?"

"Yeah, him!"

"What's he doing back here? And why would he be arguing with Chloe?"

"I don't know but I'll find out."

I quickly altered the video to only show their fight. I also tried to adjust the volume so we could hear what they were fussing about. There was another way that I could get away with this and get Jeremy out of jail, if I framed Michael. I told Cadence about the video and showed her the next day. She, James, and William then launched their mission to get Michael behind bars. And I was free.

Physically, I was free. But my heart was chained in knots. All my life, my parents seemed unmoved by their wrongdoings. But that gene must have skipped me. I was overwhelmed with guilt. I didn't get a break from the tormenting thoughts. Chloe was in the ICU fighting for her life. Jeremey was behind bars. Michael was being blamed. And it was all my fault.

I was hoping that Michael's investigation would be enough to get Jeremey out of jail. But it wasn't. Unknown number would frequently text me threatening to expose me if I didn't act. I asked my dad for 700 dollars. I lied and said there was something wrong with my car and it would cost that much to fix. He gave it to me without hesitation and I used that money to bail Jeremey out of jail. Jeremey wasn't off the hook completely, but I figured it would get unknown number off my back and it did.

But, just like my father's affairs, the truth always has a way of rearing its ugly head. When the cops came knocking at my door asking for DNA testing, I knew it was over. Before they took the sample, I confessed everything. I knew I was going to jail, but it felt so good to admit. I spent a few hours in jail feeling relieved. I prayed to God for forgiveness. I prayed harder for Chloe. I prayed for her healing. I prayed for her happiness. And I prayed that God would place in her heart forgiveness for me as well. I was a fool to think her vulnerability was my opportunity. I should have denied her advancement, stopped her from taking drugs, and been the shoulder she needed to cry on. I should have been the friend she needed me to be that night instead of the lover I wanted to be.

Both of my parents came to bail me out of jail, and they never did anything together. They were both upset, but they handled it differently.

"They have no right to charge you for this bogus charge. It was consensual!" dad yelled.

"She was inebriated so it doesn't matter," I responded.

"I'm sure if I give her parents enough money, they will drop the case."

"Chloe is not money hungry."

"Everyone has their price, son."

"We can get out of this without paying that family a dime" my mom proclaimed. "From what I hear little Ms. Chloe is pregnant with someone else's child. Apparently, she sleeps around a lot. Plus, her mom was a drug addict and a prostitute. It will be easy to tear her character apart in front of a jury. When we're done with the Wilcox family, they'll be the ones paying us. A defamation of character countersuit could pay out nicely. I've got a few lawyer friends in the PTA. I'll make sure they get on this right away."

"Mom, Chloe is not like that!"

"Ha! It doesn't matter if she's like that or not. It matters what we can prove in court."

"I don't want to do that to her," I mumbled.

"Excuse me, Joshua. Did you just say you don't want to? She's trying to get you thrown in jail. You need to do all you can do to prove your innocence. Your future depends on this."

"I'm not innocent!"

There was a moment of silence. Then my dad turned to my mom and said, "Don't worry honey, He will come to his senses soon."

Chapter 18 – Cadence's Winter 2019

"5…4…3…2…1! Happy New Year!" Daniel, Dad, and I yelled as we watched the ball drop. I pretended to be excited, but I hurt that Chloe wasn't there to celebrate. A few weeks had passed since our little group prayer, and I was strategically dipping and dodging my dad's follow up questions.

"So, what's your New Year's resolution Cadence? To start living a straight life?" Daniel teased.

"That's not funny. Your sister is not gay, and I wish you'd stop joking around like that," dad rebuked him.

"Oh, she's not?"

I rolled my eyes but didn't say anything. Dad looked at me waiting for my response.

"Cadence?" dad tried to influence me to respond. But I didn't. I looked at the ground in shame.

"See told ya!" Daniel gloated.

"Cadence, you aren't engaging in…unnatural behaviors, are you?"

"If you mean homosexual behaviors, yes. I am. But what you consider unnatural is very natural to me."

Daniel smiled so hard you could see his wisdom teeth. He was happy to not be the center of negative attention for a change. Dad gasped at my response then he looked at Daniel noticing his intrigue in the moment. "Daniel, go to your room!" dad yelled.

"What? But why?"

"Because this doesn't concern you. Now go." Daniel stomped up the stairs like a two-year old. When he was out of earshot, dad continued, "Cadence, what's going on?"

"I'm a lesbian, Dad."

"You're a lesbian, or you're curious about sleeping with women?"

"I'm attracted to girls. I have known for years. I just never said anything. But now, I have a girlfriend. Her name is Jamie and she is…"

"You can't believe what you are doing is right. What about Sodom and Gomorrah? God burned down two whole cities because of their homosexual acts and you're telling me you want to be a lesbian?"

"Not want to be…I am a lesbian."

"Well can't you choose to be straight instead?"

"You think I chose this? If I had a choice, I would not choose homosexuality. Having to face the prejudice, the criticism, and the condemnation. I didn't choose this. This is just who I am."

"No. This is not who you are. You are a God-fearing Bible-toting, good-doing, Christian girlie-girl. You're not butch. You don't like sports or fishing or hunting. You don't even look gay. You've got long hair, make-up, and dresses for God's sake."

"What do you think lesbians are supposed to look like? You think we're all the same? You think we all have short hair, wear boy's clothes, and do masculine activities? No. Lesbian is my sexual orientation. But I am still me. I'm still a bubbly, girlie, do-gooder. And I'm still Christian."

"Christian, huh," he scoffed, "What about Leviticus 18:22? Romans 1: 26-27? 1 Timothy 1:10? All Bible verses condemning homosexuality."

"That's just the way that you interpret it. If you go directly to the Hebrew and Greek words, you'd know those verses are condemning rape, pedophilia, and erotic pagan rituals. Not a loving consensual relationship."

"Interpretation!? What about do not dishonor your father? Is there a different interpretation for that? No? Didn't think so. You not only dishonor me, but you are a disgrace to me."

I was too hurt to speak. My only response was the tears that ran down my face. I wished Chloe were there.

"Interpret this Cadence, either you stop with this gay shit, or you get out of my house."

I turned to storm out of the room.

"Oh no, Cadence. You are not getting out that easily. Call her!" he handed me my cell phone which had been laying on the table.

"Huh?"

"Jamie! Call her now. Tell her it is over. Or else, get out of my house." I turned to walk away. I didn't think he was serious. But if he was going to threaten, I was going to call his bluff. "Where are you going?" he shouted.

"I'm going to get my stuff and move out of your house. No point in staying somewhere I'm not welcomed."

"Stuff? What stuff?" my dad asked.

"I'm packing up all my stuff from my room and I'm getting out of this house."

"Oh no, that stuff in your room. Your clothes, your phone," he said snatching the phone from my grasp. "Your car, your coat, shoes…None of that is your stuff. All that stuff is mine. I paid for it and when you move out, you're leaving all *my* stuff behind."

Stubbornly I walked coatless and shoeless into the cold. I angrily marched down the street determined to make it to Chloe's house seven miles away from my own. I was sure Mr. William would let me crash there. My anger gave me warmth initially. But as my anger started to fade, my feet began to freeze. I made it three blocks before turning around and giving in to my father's demands. When I walked in, he dangled my phone in my face and smiled knowing he was victorious. I grabbed the phone, called Jamie, and said, "Jamie, I can no longer date you." I didn't give an explanation. She tried to retaliate, but dad took the phone and hung up on her. He walked away stating, "You're grounded for three weeks."

Jamie approached me two days later when we got back to school. She wanted to know why I ended our relationship, especially since it seemed to be going so well. I was too ashamed to tell her that I was not bold enough to stand up to my family. "It's just not working," I said.

She read right through that, "Bullshit! It's someone else, isn't it?"

"No."

"It's Chloe. You're so wrapped up in her drama you have no time for us."

"No, I love Chloe, but I always make an effort to spend time with you despite whatever she's going through."

"Your family? They forbid us, didn't they? I saw how your brother reacted when he saw us together. I heard what he said."

"Look, I just can't be with you!" I yelled.

At home, I didn't talk to my family. I didn't eat. I didn't cry. I just stayed in my room with my door shut. Dad and Daniel both tried to reach out to me. They often knocked at my door offering my favorite foods or activities. I declined every time. Dad even gave me my phone back as a peace offering. I took the phone but still didn't talk to him.

My phone vibrated as I laid on my bed looking up to the ceiling praying for God's grace and mercy.

"Hello," I answered.

"Hey, it's James. Chloe is awake."

"What?" I sat straight up.

"Yeah, she's awake. Get down here!"

I jumped out of bed, grabbed my keys, and raced to the hospital without telling my dad where I was going. Chloe was awake and disconnected from her breathing machine. But she was groggy. When I walked into her room, she gave me a sleepy but genuine smile and a weak wave.

"She's awake but she still needs her rest," William stated.

I walked over to her and grabbed her hand, "Hey Chloe."

"Hey, my love," she labored to speak.

"Don't worry we got the guy who did this," William proudly announced.

Chloe sat up straight in her bed, "What guy?"

"Joshua."

"Joshie?"

"Yeah, he drugged you and ...uh, took advantage of you. Do you remember anything that happened?"

"Some but..."

"It would be helpful for his prosecution if for you could give your statement to the police as soon as possible. But not today. You get your rest today."

"But..."

"Rest," he responded sternly. Chloe settled back in bed and closed her eyes. William whispered to me, "The police were here earlier. They said Joshua confessed, and all they need now is Chloe's statement. I asked them to return tomorrow. I figured Chloe wouldn't be geared up for questioning today. Can you be here tomorrow too? Your statement may help as well."

"Sure! So, Joshua, is he in jail now?"

"No, he's out on bail. But I'm going to talk to some friends and see if we can get his hearing moved up. I want that monster behind bars as soon as possible." I could see the disdain in Williams eyes. My heart matched his look, not only because Joshua hurt my friend but also because he was my friend, and he betrayed my trust.

"What about Jeremey?"

"Also, out on bail. He's being prosecuted for possession of controlled substances with intent to distribute and sell."

I nodded my head. I was hurting for my friends, but things were finally coming to a head.

The next day I got to the hospital before the police did. Chloe was moved from the ICU to the stepdown unit. The room was less sterile and more cozy. William was already there he still carried the anger in his eyes, but it was a different kind of anger. Worry was intertwined.

"What's up?" I asked.

"Chloe doesn't want to testify," he muttered through clenched teeth.

"Excuse me?"

"She said it wasn't rape." I looked at Chloe who was wide awake and smiling like nothing had ever happened.

"Chloe," I spoke to her. "I know you don't want to get Joshie in trouble because he's your friend, but he hurt you. If you don't come forward, he will continue to hurt other women in the future."

"No, it's not that. He really didn't rape me. I chose to take those drugs, and I came onto him."

"Do you realize that admitting something like that can ruin your future?" William stood up and fussed. "How are you going to get into a good college with a history of drug abuse on your record?"

"How will they know?" she responded.

"Ummm, you've been absent from school because of this little hospitalization for three months. How else are you going to explain that to the college admission boards?"

"I...uh...I don't know. I guess I'll tell them the truth. Hey, I could use it to my advantage. Let them know that it was a learning experience. That it was a mistake I made, paid the consequences for, and learned to never do again."

"You think that's going to fly!" he yelled.

"Please Mr. William, calm down," I interjected.

James cheerfully walked into the room carrying balloons and flowers, "Hey everyone! Hey Chloe." He leaned over and gave a still smiling Chloe a kiss on the cheek.

"Thanks James," she responded. "Hey Cadence, have you met my brother?"

I grinned and nodded at her. "Hey James."

There was tension in the room and James could sense it. "What's going on?"

"Chloe won't testify," William said.

"There's nothing to testify. There's no crime. Joshie is innocent," she responded.

"Innocent?" James questioned. "Chloe are you sure? I mean, you did have a lot of drugs in your system. Are you sure you remember adequately?"

"My memory is just fine, and I am telling you…" A knock on the door interrupted her. It was two police officers preparing to take her statement.

"Come in," James said.

"I want to drop the charges," stated Chloe. Both officers looked at William confused. "We're not dropping any charges. Chloe give your statement," William demanded.

"I have no statement to give," she defiantly stated. Her smile disappeared.

"It doesn't matter if you try to drop the charges or not. Rape is a felony, and we have all the evidence we need. The state will still prosecute."

"Fine, I'll give my statement. But I only want Cadence in the room with me."

"No absolutely not. You are still a minor, and I refuse to have you questioned by police without my presence."

James placed a hand on William's shoulder, "Come on Mr. William, we can wait right outside. I'll stand with you."

"But…" William started to contend then resigned. He reluctantly walked out of the room guided by James.

"So, Ms. Chloe Wilcox, can you tell us what happened on Friday, November 9th at the residence of Jeremey Jones?"

Chloe looked at me, grabbed my hand, and spoke, "I was depressed. I just found out my birth mother died, and I was pregnant and alone." She turned and mouthed to me, "Sorry I didn't tell you." I patted her hand letting her know that I understood, and all was well. She continued, "My boyfri…the father of the child wanted me to get an abortion. I was supposed to meet his father, Mr. Harris at the clinic the week before to get the procedure done. I couldn't go through with it. So, Michael, he came down and confronted me at the party." Tears welled in Chloe's eyes, but she continued. "He accused me of trying to trap him…of trying to get him to marry me. He called me worthless. Said that I was…a ho and that no man in their right mind would take me as a wife, especially not him. When he left, I was furious, hurt, scared. I took every drug I could to make the pain go away. Joshua, he was just trying to check on me and make sure I was okay. But I took advantage of his kindness. I wanted revenge on Michael. I wanted him to hurt as much as he hurt me. So, I used Joshua. I came onto him. I slept with him and…and…that's all I remember."

"So, this was not rape? This was consensual?" one of the officers asked.

"Yes, purely consensual. I chose to take drugs. I chose to have sex with Joshua. And I was well aware of both of my decisions without influence from anyone or anything."

The cops nodded their heads, "Ms. Wilcox, thanks for your cooperation." Then they left.

Chloe turned to me with tears still forming, "I lost the baby, didn't I?"

I nodded my head. "Yes, I am so sorry." We both cried and held each other. I always knew Chloe was a strong girl, but to go through all of that and survive, she was elephant strong. It took strength to be honest despite all that she was risking. It took strength to stand up to her father and do the right thing. It took strength to go through the pain of a lost mother, a lost lover, and a lost baby all at the same time. I admired all that she was and all that she survived.

Chapter 19 – Chloe's Spring in 2019

Three months out of school had really put a dent in my 4.0 grade point average. Because of my one night of drinking and drugs, I ran the risk of not being able to graduate. I had to do triple the work to make up for my absence. But within three months of being back in school I was able to boost my GPA back up to a 3.5. It wasn't perfect but I was proud of my accomplishment. I wasn't sure if it was enough to get me into NYU. I stood at my locker holding the letter from NYU in my hand. My heart tossed and turned at the fact that I could be holding an acceptance or a rejection letter. My life had been full of rejections. You'd think I'd be more comfortable with it but instead of comfort I felt compound.

"Hey you!" Cadence spoke as she approached me.

"Hey," I murmured.

"You okay?"

I handed her the letter.

"Oh my God, NYU! This is what you wanted! Open it!"

I looked at her sideways. I couldn't open it. I was too anxious. My palms were sweating, my heart was racing, and I felt faint.

"I can't"

"Yes, you can," she tried to hand me the letter, but I held myself tighter and shook my head. "Want me to open it?" she asked. I nodded.

She opened the letter and started to read out loud, "Dear Chloe Wilcox, I am pleased to inform you that the Committee on Admissions has admitted you to New York University…Ahhh!" Cadence screamed and jumped around. In realizing that my dreams were coming true I matched her excitement.

"Oh my God! You're going to NYU." She continued to read, "As you know we had several candidates this year. But it was your stellar essay that put you over the top…What did you write in your essay?"

"I wrote about you," I winked at Cadence.

"Yeah right!"

"Seriously. I wrote about how you went from being in denial about racism to being one of my biggest advocates."

Cadence smiled, "NYU! You made it girl. I am so proud of you." She hugged me snugly.

"Oh, so this is why you broke up with me," Jamie's hostile voice interrupted our embrace. "You fucking her?"

Cadence grimaced, "No she's my best…"

"You fucking broke up with me for this piece of shit. This nigger ain't even worthy enough to shine my shoes," Jamie said as she pushed me into my locker. Before I could even respond Cadence cocked back her arm and executed a solid punch to Jamie's temple.

"What did you say bitch?" Cadence yelled all kinds of profanities as she delivered punch after punch. "Don't you ever speak to her like that. I will fucking kill you."

"Oh my God!" I was shocked. Being called a nigger and pushed had my mind in a different dimension. It took me a while to realize that Cadence was really fucking Jamie up. I had never seen the violent side of her. I thought she was all unicorns and rainbows. But at that moment she was Uzis and Rambos.

"Oh my God, Cadence! Cadence stop!" I yelled as I tried to pull her off of Jamie. Cadence continued to kick punch and grab, but I held her back enough that Jamie was able to escape the attack.

"You're gonna pay for this bitch!" Jamie yelled as she ran off.

"Oh my God, Cadence! Are you okay?"

"Yeah! You?"

"I'm fine," I snickered. "You beat that girl's ass! Daammmmmnnnn! I didn't know you were so…so…gangsta!" She smirked as she brushed the dust from her clothes.

Bang! Pop! We heard outside. People who were already gathered to witness Jamie's beat down started running toward the front door with increased excitement. "Oh shit!" we heard one guy say. "It's getting all fucked up!"

We followed the crowd and ran outside to the parking lot where we saw Jamie on the roof of Cadence's car with a bat. She had already smashed in the passenger's side door and mirror. We arrived just in time to see her raise the bat over her head and come down hard smashing the front window.

"What the hell are you doing you crazy bitch!?" Cadence shouted as she moved to approach and restrain Jamie. I grabbed her arm to prevent her from going. Jamie was angry and irrational. I didn't want Cadence getting hurt in the process. Jamie jumped from the roof to the hood and delivered blow after blow on the hood and headlights. I called the police on my cellphone and reported the crime. Before they arrived, Jamie fled the scene. The police took our statements, arranged for the car to be towed, and escorted us to Cadence's house.

Mr. Ellison was standing at the front door when we arrived. "Cadence! What happened to your car?"

"Jamie happened to my car."

"What the…" he gawked at the damage after it was dropped off in the driveway. "See, that's what happens when you fool around with the devil."

"God, Dad! I am really not in the mood for this," Cadence rolled her eyes and started to walk up the stairs.

"Hi Mr. Ellison," I said trying to break up the tension respectfully.

"Chloe," he answered through clenched teeth. I had always been polite to Mr. Ellison, but I don't think he really liked me very much. He looked at me like he thought I was a bad influence on Cadence. I was pleasantly surprised when Cadence told me he came to the hospital to pray for me. Hoped that it would make us closer. But he seemed to dislike me even more after my recovery.

"Cadence!" He continued to fuss, "I don't care if you're in the mood or not. Turn around and look at me when I talk to you." Cadence obliged. "You and this homosexual shit has brought destruction into this house. Now I talked to our pastor and he, thank God, is willing to pray over your soul and bring an end to this abomination."

"You did what?"

"We need to pray for your healing. You need to turn from your wicked ways, repent, and live a good wholesome life. Get married, have some babies, make me proud."

"I want to get married, have babies, and make you proud. But I plan to do those things with a woman."

Mr. Ellison laughed, "You're being ridiculous! How can you have babies with a woman? It's not natural."

"Adoption. In-vitro. I don't know. All I do know is that is what I want."

"What you want? God doesn't care about what you want. He cares that you are saved and holy which means giving up this ridiculous LGB…T…LMNOP lifestyle."

"You know what? I can't do this anymore." Cadence handed Mr. Ellison her keys, "I can't live a lie. I am who I am, and I do not need to hide it or deny it for you."

"Hide? Deny? I'm not asking you to hide anything. You need to change, and you can change it if you have enough faith. Anything can be done for those who believe in Our Lord Jesus Christ. You know that."

"Yes, I know it. God is almighty and can do anything. But maybe it's not in His will to change me. You don't think I prayed for this already? I prayed almost every day since I was 12. I wanted more than anything for God to change me. But He didn't. This is me. This is who He intended me to be."

"A sin? God didn't intend for you to live a life of sin!"

"Well either I live as a lie, or I live as a lesbian. Either way it is a sin." Cadence took her shoes off, took her jacket off, handed them to Mr. Ellison and walked out the door. Mr. Ellison was speechless. I followed Cadence.

"I'll get us a Lyft," I said as I took off my jacket to share with her.

"Thanks." I could feel her pain radiating off her body like steam though she was quiet and staring off in the other direction, I knew she felt comfort in me being there.

"I'm so proud of you," I whispered in her ear. She looked at me, halfway smiled, and hugged me. A few tears escaped both of our eyes. We straightened when our Lyft pulled up.

When we got to my house, I decided I was going to request Cadence stay with us and I wasn't going to take no for an answer from my dad. I walked into the living room where he was sitting and watching TV. "Dad!" I said, "Cadence is a lesbian, her dad kicked her out the house, and she's staying here with us."

He stood up, looked at the both of us, and said, "Okay." Then he embraced us both in his arms, kissed us each on the top of the head and sat back down like it was just any other ordinary day.

Cadence was two sizes smaller than me, but I shared all my clothes and shoes with her. "We'll go to the mall tomorrow and get you some clothes," I said when she walked out of the bathroom in my nightgown that hung loosely."

"Thanks. I appreciate it."

She laid down and cried. Sometimes there are no words big enough to comfort a pain that strong. I laid behind her and held her as she wept. I figured she wouldn't want to go to school the next morning, but she was up, dressed, and ready before I was. There was a lot of talk around the hallways of the big fight and the car vandalism. For those who were not there, they were able to view the incidents all over social media, compliments of our classmates who stood back and recorded on their smart phones instead of trying to help. Cadence got a lot of praise for her role in the conflict. But every high-five and acknowledgement made her more uncomfortable.

"Look at you, Miss Popular huh," I said after the seventh person called Cadence out.

"It doesn't feel right… getting praise for a fight, for my destroyed car…"

"Hey, Cadence, heard you came out the closet! Congratulations!" one of the Sophomore boys yelled at her.

"…or for coming out of the closet," Cadence continued while rolling her eyes.

"I think it's awesome! You fought to defend me. Jamie was way out of line and you stepped in and let her know that she could not treat me like that. And your official coming out party…well I'm sure that paved the way for others who have been too afraid to be themselves," I said as I pointed to that Sophomore boy who started kissing his boyfriend.

"Wow!" Cadence said giggling. "And here I thought I was the only one."

I laughed and shook my head. Then Cadence's countenance changed from laughter to a scowl.

"Hey Chloe," I heard Joshua's voice from behind me. My heart started beating fast. We hadn't spoken since Jeremey's party. If I happened to see him passing in the hallway he'd often run in the opposite direction. I didn't know if he was mad, hurt, or just feeling guilty. I only felt guilt and shame. "Hi Cadence," he acknowledged.

"Joshua," she murmured. I slowly turned around, unsure what to expect. Unsure how I would feel when I faced my old friend after our night of drugs, sex, and near-death experiences. But when I looked at him, all I felt was love. He was still my friend. We both made mistakes that night. But that is all it was, a mistake. Something to learn from.

"Hi Joshi…Joshua."

"I am so sorry for what I've done."

"You didn't do anything. We both decided to sleep with each other that night."

"Yeah but I left you…"

"All is forgiven," I interrupted. He looked skeptical. "Look, we both were intoxicated that night. We both weren't thinking straight. It's water under the bridge. We are good."

"We're good?"

"Yeah!"

"Oh, okay well…I guess…I'll see you around?"

"You will," I smiled then Cadence and I walked away.

"You may forgive him, but I don't," Cadence mentioned. "He was supposed to take care of you that night, not abandon you."

"He was drunk. He was scared, I get it."

"No excuse!"

"It's not healthy holding onto such hate. You need to forgive him too."

"Maybe one day. But not today!"

I giggled and shook my head.

Sunday morning, I woke to Cadence getting dolled up. She put on a cute pink dress and navy-blue shoes. "You going to church?" I asked surprised.

"Yeah!" Cadence responded.

"But…your dad, the people…they are all going to judge you."

"I'm not going to let their backlash prevent me from developing my relationship with Jesus. I need Jesus now more than ever. Wanna go?"

"Naw, maybe next week." I rolled over and went back to sleep.

I woke to the sounds of a sermon coming from the living room, "Aren't you glad that He's a forgiving Father! Aren't you glad that He's a loving Father! Aren't you glad that He's a healing father! Hallelujah…" I crept down the stairs and saw William watching a sermon on TV and nodding his head in agreement with the words.

"Hey dad."

He paused the TV and turned around to look at me, "Hey Chloe. You doing okay?"

"Yeah, you woke me."

"Oh. Well, you want to come join me?"

"Naw."

"You know, I was wrong for leaving the church. Things are not always going to work out the way we want them too. But they work out alright. God is a good God no matter what it looks like."

"I wish I could believe that."

"What do you mean wish?"

"God, Love, Religion…how can I believe any of that? My life is shit! I'm nothing but a piece of shit! Oh, uh…sorry…for my language." William brushed my swearing off and urged me to continue. "I mean why would God make me like this?"

"Like what exactly?"

"Ugly, unwanted, unloved, tormented. You say He's a loving God. You say He's good. Then why would he allow me to be raped at five? Why would He allow Michael to break my heart? Why would He allow Cadence to be chastised and abandoned? Why would He allow my baby, my mother, and Bianca to die? What kind of good God allows that? Either He's not all powerful or He's not all good."

"Ugly? Unwanted? How could you think that about yourself?"

"Cause it's true! I mean look at me. My skin, my hair, who wants me? I thought Michael wanted me. But he made it plenty clear that I am not worthy of his love."

William sighed and looked down. "I failed you. I had the opportunity to show you that God is good through the storm and through the sunshine. The rain seems bad when you are going through it. But in all truth, it comes not to destroy but to cleanse, to quench, and to help you grow. The good things and the bad things that happen in our life all have purpose. The purpose is of benefit for our good even if it doesn't seem that way. I don't have the answers for why all the bad things that happened to you did but I can see the silver lining in some. You lost a baby. I can only imagine what a horrible pain that is. But the father of your child is an idiot. He was too dumb to see that he had the most beautiful person in the world - you. One day a man is going to come around who is smart enough to recognize you for what you truly are, a beautiful woman of God. You being molested at such a young age was horrible. It is something no child should have to go through. But it led you to me. And you are the most wonderful thing to ever happen to me. Chloe, you are not a piece of shit. You are a masterpiece. You were carefully constructed by an all-powerful, all-mighty, all-loving God.

You are loved, needed, wanted, talented, delightful, and wonderfully made."

I heard his words, but I had trouble believing them.

Chapter 20 – Cadences' Monsoon in 2019

"Turn with me to John chapter11 verse 3, when you have it say amen," Pastor Charles spoke with authority while standing at the pulpit. I decided to drive an hour north to attend his church. Him showing up to the ICU to pray for Chloe intrigued me.

"Amen!" I exclaimed with several other enthusiastic followers when I reached the correct verse.

"I'm reading from the ESV version…So the sisters, referring to Mary and Martha, sent to him, saying, 'Lord, he whom you love is ill.' But when Jesus heard it, he said, 'This illness does not lead to death. It is for the glory of God, so that the Son of God may be glorified through it.' You see there? Jesus already knew that Lazarus was not going to die from this illness. He knew that He was going to resurrect him, and all would see and believe that Jesus was the real Messiah. Okay, now skip down to verse 32… Um, Cadence, can you read that verse for us?"

"Sure!" I responded humbled that he remembered my name and though I a guest at his church still called on me to share in the reading of the word, "Now when Mary came to where Jesus was and saw him, she fell at his feet, saying to him, 'Lord, if you had been here, my brother would not have died."

"Mmm, hmmm, keep going."

"When Jesus saw her weeping, and the Jews who had come with her also weeping, he was deeply moved in his spirit and greatly troubled. And he said, 'Where have you laid him?' They said to him, 'Lord, come and see. Jesus wept."

"Okay, stop right there," interrupted Pastor. "Jesus wept. Jesus what now church? Jesus…"

"Wept!" we responded.

"Now why would Jesus weep? Jesus knew that Lazarus was sick. Jesus knew that he was going to die. Jesus knew that Lazarus' sisters, Mary, and Martha, were going to be hurt. Jesus knew He had the power and the will to bring Lazarus back to life. Jesus knew all this. He knows all. So why was He weeping? John 11:35, it is the shortest verse in the Bible, Jesus wept, but it says so much. He wept because his friends, Mary and Martha were hurting. Jesus loved Mary and Martha. He loved them the same way he loves you. He cares when you are hurting. He cares about your feelings. When you hurt, He hurts. When you cry, He cries. Cast all your anxieties on Him. Why church?"

"Because he cares for you," several people responded.

"That's right! Because he cares for you. He cares how you feel. He cares about your thoughts, your desires, and your fears. Sometimes your thoughts are not His. Sometimes, your desires aren't in line with what you need. Sometimes your fears need to be conquered. But He cares, nevertheless. He hears you when you pray and empathizes with you when you hurt. But sometimes you have to go through the pain to get the glory. Sometimes our prayers are not answered, not because He doesn't love us or doesn't care. But maybe because He has greater plans. Lazarus died. Mary and Martha cried. They all felt pain. But they had to go through that pain so that Jesus could show the world who He really is. So that He could demonstrate His power and authority. So that all would know, believe, and be saved."

My dad isn't right. God does care about my feelings. The thought continued to play in my head. *He loves me. He cares about my hurts, my wants, and my needs. I tried to conceal my truth thinking God didn't care. I tried to stop being a lesbian. I tried to deny it. I tried to ignore it. I tried to pray it away. Then when I finally accepted it, I lost my family. That hurt. But God cares and there is a reason why he has not answered my prayer. There is a reason why my family is not there. I don't know what the reason is, but I have faith and believe that whatever it is, my pain will end with His glory.*

Service was so moving I borrowed Mr. Wilcox's car and made the same long trip that next Sunday and the Sunday after that. I asked Chloe to join me each time, but she politely refused. I decided not to give up on her, nor to push her. I just prayed that she would soon come to Jesus. As we got closer to graduation, Chloe's spiritual curiosity gradually grew.

"So, you know Jesus?" she asked one night as we were getting ready for bed.

"Yeah," I smiled.

"What's he like?"

"He's kind, He's smart, He's caring, He's understanding, He's forgiving, He loves me so much, and I love Him too."

"How can you love Him? You've never even seen Him."

"I may not have seen Him, but I feel Him."

Chloe looked at me confused, "I don't get it."

"You remember when you were pregnant? You never saw your unborn child, but you knew he was there, inside of you, and without even knowing him, meeting him, or seeing him, you loved him correct?"

She didn't answer but she nodded like she got it.

"So why is there so much evil in the world? I mean if God exist, and He created everything, why would he even create evil? Why would He let good people suffer?" Chloe asked during season 1 episode 3 of *The Umbrella Academy*.

I paused the TV. "God is always good. He made us all with the hopes that we would choose to be with Him, love Him, obey, and follow Him. But He didn't want to create us as little unthinking robots. He made us with a free will. And some people has used their free will to do evil things."

"Yeah, but why don't they just get punished? Instead we all have to suffer for their crap?"

"They do get punished. You may never see their consequences but every action we make has one. And yes, it is unfortunate that sometimes we get hurt because others choose to do evil. But God is there. Anything that He allows to happen to us, He knows we can not only handle it, but we can grow from it. We can learn from it. We can get stronger from it. Our faith and our relationship with Him can develop from it. Even evil, God uses it and changes it so that it all works out for our good."

"How is Jesus God and man? If Jesus is God, who is God the father? How is the father and the son both God if there is only one God? And how is the word made flesh and the flesh is Jesus? And where does the Holy Spirit fit in all this?" she asked one morning over breakfast.

"Well, look at me," I stood up, "I am one person, right? I'm Cadence Alexandria Ellison. There is only one of me, right?"

"Yeah!"

"But I've got an arm and a leg and a hand and a head, right?"

"Uh huh."

"Better yet, I've got a mind, a body, and a soul, right?"

"Uh huh."

"But it is still all me. Just like God. He is not one dimensional. He is one God but has several different parts. God the father is the all-mighty inexplicable powerful mind. Jesus is the relatable humanly touchable part of God – the body. And the Holy Spirit, well she is the part that lives inside of you – the soul. And the word, that's what God says. That's His voice. That's how God communicates. He communicates through the Bible or directly to you."

She nodded though I wasn't sure if she really understood what I was saying.

"You've been thinking about this a lot, huh?"

"Not really."

"Mmm hmm, why don't you just come with me to church?"

"Maybe one day. But I'm just not ready yet?"

"Ready?"

"Yeah, I'm not holy enough to go to church. I'll probably get struck by lightning as soon as I enter the building."

I giggled. "You don't have to get ready to go to church. You just go. If any of us waited until we were *good enough* to go to church, no one would ever go. We've all got issues. We have all sinned. We all need healing. But you can't heal yourself. You've gotta go to Jesus for that."

Chloe still declined my invite to church that Sunday. Nevertheless, I kept praying for her.

**

I walked down the hallway of my high school and out the front door for the last time. Chloe was already outside sitting on a bench reading a book.

"Well haven't we come full circle. On the first day of school I saw you sitting here, reading a book, and waiting for your dad to pick you up. And on the last day of school, I see you here, sitting, reading and waiting for your dad to pick you up."

Chloe giggled, "only this time you're waiting with me." She scooted over so that I could sit next to her. "It sucks that my dad still won't give me a car."

"Well you can't have a car on campus at NYU first year anyway."

"True, true!"

I was excited about our future. I didn't get accepted into NYU, but I did manage to get into Manhattan Community College.

Chloe and I were planning to move into a cute little two bedroom flat in Brooklyn.

I pulled out a book for myself and started reading knowing it would be a while before Mr. Wilcox got out of court. He was working on a volatile child neglect case which drained his time and his energy. I was captivated in the hot and steamy night between the main character and her new lover when I heard, "Beep-Beep!" I recognized the sound of the horn and looked up to see what used to be my car. It was completely fixed up, painted, and cleaned. I was excited to see my car back to its full glory. But upset knowing it was no longer my car. My dad was in the driver's seat smiling and waving. Behind him, driving his own dodge charger was Daniel. He didn't look at me. He sat in the car looking angry and mumbling. I frowned at dad as he got out of the car and approached me.

"Hi Mr. Ellison!" Chloe spoke.

He smiled. "Hi Chloe. Heard you're going to New York for school next year."

"Yes sir! And Cadence will be joining me."

He looked surprised. "To NYU?"

"No," I chimed in. "I'll be at Manhattan Community."

"Community? You could go to a school near here if you wanted to go to a community college."

"Naw, I want to be as far away from here as possible."

"I take that to mean you want to be far away from me?"

I shrugged acknowledging that he said it, but I was thinking it.

"Cadence, I miss you." He should have thought of that before he kicked me out the house. I didn't say anything; my facial expression did all the talking for me. He continued, "You being a lesbian…it's not the life I want for you. But I'd rather have you in my life as a lesbian than not in my life at all. Cadence, I love you. You and your brother, you guys are my world. You are all I have left. All I want is what is best for you. I just want you to live a happy and full life." I didn't speak. "Well, anyway, I think this belongs to you." He tossed me the keys and started to walk away.

"But, Dad, you said that this was your car. That I owned nothing," I called to him.

"I was wrong. I was wrong about a lot of things. I apologize. The car was a gift for your 16th birthday. It is still yours. Just know that I love you. I love you no matter what." He gave me a hug, kissed my cheek then hoped into the car with Daniel who drove away without even acknowledging my presence.

Chloe approached me from behind, "Well, you got your car back." She smiled.

"Better than that, I got my dad back."

"Your brother's still acting like an ass I see."

"Yeah but that's his problem. I'm not going to live my life worried about what other people think. The only thing that matters is what God thinks of me. That was the message I got in church last week. Which by the way, you are still welcome to come with me, if you want."

"Mmm. I'll think about it." Chloe called her dad and let him know he needn't worry about picking us up.

Saturday was graduation. I was happy to see my dad in the front row clapping, cheering, and whistling as I walked across the stage. Daniel decided not to come. It stung but I realized, that was his loss, and not mine.

On Sunday I got up, got dressed, and made myself some scrambled eggs and bacon for breakfast.

"You ready?" Chloe said as she came into the kitchen then popped a piece of bacon in her mouth.

"For what?" I asked.

"For church! I'm coming with you."

"Really!?" I was so happy God answered that prayer.

"Yeah, let's go. Don't want to be late." I grabbed my keys, and we were off.

"You think God's proud of you?" Chloe asked as we drove up I-95.

"I hope so. I try to do good."

"Hmm," she said. "You think He's proud of me?"

"I know God loves you very much and He wants to be a part of your life."

"Hmm."

We entered church and found a spot near where James was seated. He was on his feet singing and waving along with the choir. He waved to us as we entered. A few people recognized Chloe and waved to her or gave her hugs and told her how good it was to see her. You could see her discomfort with all the affection she was getting.

Pastor Charles took to the alter. He lovingly nodded at us then proceeded, "Turn your Bibles to Exodus chapter 3." The chapter told the story of Moses at the burning bush. God spoke to Moses and told him to free the Israelites from slavery. Moses responded, "Who am I that I should bring the Israelites out of Egypt?"

Pastor then started to point out Moses' background, "Moses was an orphan. He spoke with a stutter. He was a runaway. And he was a wanted murderer. Because of his past and his shortcomings, Moses felt apprehensive about his destiny. He questioned why God would choose him of all people to complete such a ginormous task. He was insecure. Do you know what insecurity is? It is when you believe what the devil thinks of you and you don't believe what God thinks of you. The devil always seems to point out your flaws. Your too fat, your too ugly, too stupid, too incompetent, too unlikable, too untalented, your too black, your too white, your nose is too big, your ears are too big, your too short, too... oh my God, too anything. Moses thought he was too damaged. Abraham thought he was too old. Jeremiah thought he was too young. Those thoughts aren't flaws. They are the Devil's lies and manipulations. Sometimes the Devil feeds this nonsense to you through other people telling you what you are too blank to do. Sometimes he whispers these insecurities in your ear, causing anxiety and fear. But if you had more faith in what God thinks of you, you'd know that He sees you are beautiful, smart, talented, loved, and wanted. You'd know that you are unique and created with a divine purpose. You'd know that you can do all things through Christ who strengthens you. There is no burden you can't bear. No mountain you can't climb. No giant you can't defeat. No challenge you can't conquer. You'd know that you are God's treasured and highly favored."

I looked over at Chloe who had tears running down her cheeks. I gave her a hug.

"All my life," she whispered. "All my life I have felt so inadequate, so unwanted, so bad. But..."

"But you're not." I interrupted. "You are God's treasured. And I love you with all my heart. You are my best friend."

"I love you too," she said as she hugged me back.

James walked over to us. "I know you guys got room for your big brother," he joked as he put his arms around us both. We all giggled. "I love you guys too!" he playfully announced.

**

"Tell dad I'll be at the house a little later for dinner. He told me you guys are having pizza. You know I love his famous handmade pizza. Mmm, better than delivery," James shouted to us as we were getting in the car after church. Since Chloe's hospitalization, James had not missed a Sunday dinner with us. He started calling William dad and me sis. We all grew close over those trying months. Even Joshie had inched his way back into our lives. After Chloe forgave and renewed her friendship with him, it didn't take long for me to do the same. We were a family, a very odd-appearing family, but a family, nevertheless.

Postlude

I didn't grow up in the church and had no exposure to God until I went to jail. I remember when juror number one stood up and the judge asked, "On the count of rape in the first degree, what do you the jury rule?"

"Guilty," her thin pale lips asserted seemingly in slow motion. The word wore me down like a ton of bricks. For a moment, my vision went black and my hearing deafened. My shock dissolved as the sounds of my wailing mother conquered the atmosphere. I was only seventeen, and I was sentenced to life in prison.

I wasn't the best teenager. I skipped school a few times. I smoked weed a few times. But I never hurt anyone. I didn't deserve to have my entire life waste away in a cold dark cell. My life was just beginning and with a few simple mistakes, it was already over. Taylor, the girl who accused me of rape, was my girlfriend, or so I thought she was. We had been sleeping together for months before her racist ass father caught us in the act one afternoon. He freaked out and beat me so bad I ended up in the ER getting ten stitches on my forehead. It was at the hospital that he convinced Taylor to tell the police officers who were investigating my assault to say that I was raping her. As a result, Taylor's dad remained free of charges, and I left the hospital in handcuffs.

Taylor mouthed, "I'm sorry" as she watched me being hauled off by officers. Then she went about her business and I went to jail. I remember feeling so angry at the world. I blamed the jury, and the judge for not seeing through Taylor's lies. All they saw was an innocent little White girl victim against me - a big Black angry man. I blamed my ill-equipped state appointed half-assed lawyer for failing to point out the obvious. If it was not consensual, why was she on top of me when her father walked in? Why did she pick me up in her car and bring me to her house? Why weren't any of my friends who were prepared to testify that we were in a relationship called to the stand? Why did she text me that day and talk about how she wanted to fuck me? None of the evidence matched her testimony, but it all matched mine. However, America is so far gone when it comes to propaganda criminalizing Black folks that the obvious is ignored. I hated my life and all the people who were involved in contributing to my misery. I wanted so bad to kill myself those first few nights in prison. Then I met Jesus.

Jesus was my Hispanic cellmate from the Bronx. He was a bitter man who hated life even more than I did. He was a hot-headed asshole. I observed as he harassed and tortured other inmates, especially White ones. To him, White people were responsible for the destruction of his family. His mom and dad were separated from him and his siblings in a detentions center in Texas. His youngest brother died at that detention center. The pain from losing someone so close destroyed him thus he made it his mission to make others hurt as much as he did.

Troy was a frequent victim of Jesus' assaults. He was a short thin White guy who was convicted for the murder of his father who had been beating his mother for years. Jesus saw this frail man as an opportunity to obtain revenge. He often would take Troy's lunch tray and bully him into submission. Troy had to buy Jesus all kinds of crap at the commissary in exchange for not getting beat up. I felt bad for Troy. He already had a shitty life and Jesus was making it worse. But in prison, you learn quickly to keep your head down and stay out of others business; so, I didn't intervene. Until one day at breakfast, I couldn't sit silently and watch an overt injustice continue. I stood up for Troy and ended up getting jumped by Jesus and several of his buddies. It landed me in solitary where my anger festered. Taylor, her dad, the jury, and the judge were all White, and they were the reason why I was in jail. Jesus and his friends were all Hispanic, and they were the reason I was in solitary. Because of my experiences with them, I hated White people and I hated Hispanics. It's hard not to become prejudice when your only exposure to a certain group of people are bad encounters.

God tried to speak to me in solitary. I could feel him trying to tell me that White and Hispanic people were His children same as I was. I ignored Him and convinced myself that God was either an evil dictator who didn't care about my suffering or he did not exist and was merely a fabrication used by White people to make minorities less resistant to oppression. I would have lived my life angry and destroyed, no better than the people I hated, had it not been for Troy.

As soon as I was released from solitary, Troy showed his gratitude by gifting me three honeybuns. We quickly became friends. Troy was good peoples. He had a rough background, but he was super smart and despite his weak appearance, he had an unbeatable emotional and spiritual strength. I admired him and becoming friends with him caused my racist views against White people to dissipate.

Troy spent most of his days reading the Bible. It was his coping mechanism. Initially, I thought it was bullshit, but Troy insisted I try to form a relationship with God myself. I resisted picking up the Bible for three years unconvinced that a loving God existed and yet allowed Troy and I to be imprisoned in such an awful place. Then I witnessed Troy fend off seven guys without raising a fist. He accidently bumped into this big brawny dude during lunch. The guy and all his friends surrounded and threatened Troy. Troy got on his knees, pulled out his Bible and started to pray out loud. All of those guys left him alone. After that, I decided to try God too.

I borrowed Troy's book flipped it to a random page and read Galatians 3:26-28, "for in Christ Jesus you are all sons of God, through faith. For as many of you as were baptized into Christ have put on Christ. There is neither Jew nor Greek, there is neither slave nor free, there is no male and female, for you are all one in Christ Jesus And if you are Christ's, then you are Abraham's offspring, heirs according to promise." *Was God trying to tell me something?* The entire time that I was in solitary I felt like God was trying to steer me away from my anti-white racist outlook on life. And the first page from the Bible I read indicated the same thing. All those who except Jesus as their Lord and savior are children of God. No matter the color, sex, ethnicity, or situation. I immediately became intrigued and started to read more random pages.

"No, in all these things we are more than conquerors through him who loved us. For I am sure that neither death nor life, nor angels nor rulers, nor things present nor things to come, nor powers, nor height nor depth, nor anything else in all creation, will be able to separate us from the love of God in Christ Jesus our Lord. Romans 8:37-39." *Okay, that's nice. So, God's children have some power, huh. They are more than conquerors. Not only that, but God loves them so much that nothing can destroy it. I like that.*

More curious then willing, I went to Troy and asked, "Okay, so that Bible of yours got me interested. What I got to do to become Christian?"

He smiled at me, "All you have to do is believe and confess."

"Confess what?"

"That Jesus is the son of God and your Lord and Savior."

"That's it?"

"Yep."

"So how I do that?"

Troy closed his eyes, lifted his hands, and spoke, "Repeat after me." I closed one eye and looked at Troy apprehensively with the other. Animated, Troy continued, "Heavenly Father…I confess that I am a sinner…I ask for forgiveness…I believe that Jesus Christ died for my sins…rose from the dead…and is seated at the right hand of the Father… I pray that you come into my heart…and cleanse me of my wicked ways…Amen."

I repeated every word; but I had no idea what I was doing or saying. However, I trusted Troy and figured saying a few words shouldn't hurt. When Troy was done and I repeated the last word, Amen, I paused to see if heaven was going to open up and some miraculous event was going to occur. Nothing happened. I felt no difference.

"Now, if you believe in your heart the words you just said, you are saved," Troy announced. I had no idea what he meant. I shrugged my shoulders and replied, "Okay." Troy let me hold onto his Bible. He said he had others in his cell.

That night, I couldn't sleep. There was a gentle tug on my heart strings and a compulsion to open the Bible and read more. I tossed and turned trying to ignore the feeling which intensified until frustrated, I ripped off my covers and opened the book to another random page. "Therefore I tell you, whatever you ask in prayer, believe that you have received it, and it will be yours. Mark 11:24." *Hmmm, really? All I have to do is pray, and believe and it will be done, huh.* I didn't believe it but figured why not try it. I got down and I prayed that justice would prevail. That somehow, some way my illegitimate charges would be dropped, and I would be free. I prayed then I forgot about it and went on carrying out my life sentence.

Three months later, my lawyer came to visit me. She said that Taylor had gone to the DA and confessed that she lied about the rape. She petitioned to free me from jail. Apparently, Taylor was dating some girl who told her she was wrong for letting an innocent man rot in jail. Taylor had always felt guilt in her spirit but being called out by her love interest prompted her to act. It took a few months, but the prosecution dropped the charges, and I was freed.

The night I left prison, Troy stood in my cell wishing me fair well.

"You are a stronger believer than I am. Why are you still here and I am not?" I asked him.

"Cause I'm stronger than you. God knows I can handle it," he teased. He had that kind of sense of humor—one where he could make light of the darkest situations. He continued, "Besides, I actually did my crime you didn't. Whenever we do wrong, we have to pay for our consequences. I'm just paying for mine. But God is here. He is my strength and my protection. He is merciful and I know He watches over me. For you though, God has given you a second chance at life. Make sure you do good with it."

**

"I promised Troy I would, and I kept true to my word. I got my GED then went to HVAC school and got my license. I got a nice job then found a nice girl and married her. We have two beautiful kids. Through it all, I have been an active member of my church and even started a prison ministry so that I can come in here and share my story with you knuckle-heads." The small group of inmates I was mentoring at Waking Correctional Facility chuckled. "I had no idea what I was getting into when I repeated Troy's words and declared Jesus as my Lord and Savior. But it was the best decision I ever made. When I took one step toward God, he took ten towards me. My change didn't happen overnight. It was a gradual journey. But God was there guiding me, loving me, protecting me, and teaching me every step of the way. Now the Bible is my favorite past-time. And this prison ministry is my blessing. Through it, thirty-seven people in this jail alone have already given their life over to Christ. The bondage, shame, and guilt of sin no longer oppresses them. I'm not saying that when you get saved, all your problems will disappear, and you will be freed from jail automatically. But I do know that God gives your spirit and your mind freedom, peace, love, and protection. I know it's tough—being in jail, isolated, vulnerable, away from your family. But this book…" I raised up my Bible for emphasis, "This book is freedom."

Topics for discussion

Unanswered Prayers

God is good. *All the time.* And all the time. *Good is good* - A common theme in Christianity. But when your prayers go unanswered it doesn't feel this way. Little wants that we don't get, we can brush off and move on. But when it comes to large problems, the terminal illness of a spouse, miscarriage, unjust imprisonment, or murder of friends, it can be challenging to maintain faith. Reflect on 2 Corinthians 12:7-9 and Romans 8:28. How does this relate to the unanswered prayers in this novel? How does it relate in your own life? Can you think of times in your life when unanswered prayers worked out for your good?

LGBTQ+ and Christianity

Cadence is a lesbian and a Christian. She struggled with her sexual orientation and the morality associated. She continued to go to church, pray, have faith, and follow God regardless. Is homosexuality a sin? What does the Bible say about homosexuality? Is there misinterpretation? How is homosexual activity different than other sins? Why is homosexuality treated differently in the Christian church? Is a sinner going to church hypocritical or human? Why did God allow LGBTQ to exist?

Mental Health – Depression, Anxiety, Stress, Transference

Chloe and Daniel both suffer from depression and turned to drugs to cope which negatively affected their lives. William had acute stress disorder and buried himself in work to cope. However, his judgement at work was affected. His transference sent a potentially innocent man to jail. What are some better mechanisms of dealing with depression and stress? What are some barriers to getting appropriate care for mental illness? How does stigma, insecurity, costs, and resources affect people's ability to get the psychological care they need? How does stress, anxiety, depression, or transference affect our work or relationships?

Substance abuse

Maybeline, Chloe, and Daniel all had problems with drug and alcohol abuse. Addiction is a disease with risk factors including genetic predisposition, mental illness, and psychosocial traumas. In the 80s, there was a national campaign to combat this pandemic – The Say No to Drugs Campaign, which enlisted celebrities, politicians, and athletes to teach kids the dangers of drug abuse through TV shows, movies, and commercials. Today, there is a lack of effort to combat these dangers and now not only are there problems with illicit drugs but the pandemic of abuse of prescription drugs has become paramount. What are some things we as a community can do to combat prescription and illicit drug abuse?

Rape

The idea of what constitutes rape has changed significantly over the years. Initially it was thought of as forcible vaginal penetration where the female victim was required to say "no" during the encounter. However, different situations have shown that there are other sexual violations that are equally damaging. What about rape while the victim is inebriated? Rape of a minor? Rape of an adult who is mentally incapable of making decisions? What about women raping men? Men raping men? Women raping women? Coercion? Bribery? Threats? What exactly is rape? Was Chloe raped by Joshua? Or was Joshua raped by Chloe?

Racism

Chloe was one of three minorities in her high school. Besides her, there was a Hispanic female in Daniel's class and an Asian female in her class. She tried to befriend the Asian girl, but she was brushed off. Racism is not just White people's negative prejudice against Blacks. It also happens across minorities. It can happen within a race – light skin vs dark skin, poor vs rich, or slang vs articulate are some examples. It can also occur when Black people prejudge Whites. The title of this book is Cute for a Black Girl which is a backward compliment. Such compliments (smart for a Hispanic, cool for an Asian, cute for a Black) are insulting as they infer that a particular race or group is usually not smart, cool, or cute and you are only sort of smart, cool, or cute. James described Cadence as someone who can sing for a White girl. White people get it too. But is it a double standard when these things are said in reference to someone who is not a minority?

Insecurity

Many characters in the book have insecurity issues. Chloe feels insecure about her looks. Cadence feels insecure about her sexuality. Daniel feels insecure about his physical and emotional strength. Joshua feels insecure about his family and himself. How do these characters deal with these insecurities - drugs, denial, avoidance, aggression, arrogance, redirecting, misdirecting? What are some better ways to handle insecurity?

Chloe was treated differently because of her skin tone. Cadence was prejudged because of her sexual orientation. Does our environment contribute to our own insecurities?

Acknowledgements

Doctors, authors, lawyers, entrepreneurs, engineers, pharmacists, scientists, police officers, NBA players, and all other professions of this world owe their success to one profession – teachers. I am especially thankful to the teachers who have shaped and influenced my life. I want to give special thanks to my 7th and 8th grade teacher, Mr. Rybczyk for his dedication to his work and his role in my success.

Thanks to Courtney for always seeing unicorns and rainbows despite how dark the world can get. I am grateful for all the laughs we have shared together.

Thanks to Jenny and Sarah because the stories of your life gave life to this book. Thank you for being my inspiration.

Thanks to Donna, for being my mom and providing me support, understanding, and love.

Thanks to Malachi, Tianna, Tristan, Asia, Yasmeen, and Jai'den for being my crazy kids and bringing me joy and laughter.

Thanks to Damaris, Ronnelia, and Tara for being my best friends, showing me love, and for always having my back.

Thanks to Sheldon for being my ride or die companion. Life with you has been filled with excitement, adventure, friendship, and genuine love. It's been a rollercoaster of a journey and I am still enjoying the ride.

Thanks to Dea and Reggie for being my siblings and showing me strength.

And most of all, thanks to God for filling my life with so many wonderful people and blessing me with contentment.

To all those who have read this book, thank you so much for supporting my work. If you enjoyed this book, please check out my first novel "200 Letters" and my third novel, "Stepping Off the Porch."

Also, don't forget to leave a review as this is helpful for us indie authors. God Bless!

CPSIA information can be obtained
at www.ICGtesting.com
Printed in the USA
LVHW081331031021
699374LV00010B/1338